THE ULTIMATE EPILOGUE

DESPERATELY SEEKING DUKE

CAROLINE LINDEN

CAROLINE LINDEN

Desperately Seeking Duke: The Ultimate Epilogue © 2022 P.F. Belsley

About a Kiss © 2020 P.F. Belsley

Cover Design © 2022 Erin Dameron-Hill/EDHGraphics

ISBN: 979-88246725-6-5

CONTENTS

DESPERATELY SEEKING DUKE: THE ULTIMATE EPILOGUE

ABOUT A KISS

DESPERATELY SEEKING DUKE: THE ULTIMATE EPILOGUE

DEAR READER

Each book in the Desperately Seeking Duke series tells the story of a couple: Max and Bianca (About a Rogue), Drew and Ilsa (A Scot to the Heart), Will and Philippa (All the Duke I Need), as well as Agnes and Felix (How the Scot Was Won), and Kit and Jennie (About a Kiss). I wanted to tell their romances completely, and I hope readers ended each book knowing that particular couple had found their happily-ever-after.

But.

This *series* is about more than three couples with a common name. It has always been about a family—a family who suffered terrible losses and heartaches as well as immense joy and love. A family led by an indomitable woman trying to navigate increasingly difficult and heartrending circumstances, and mostly succeeding, simply because she would not allow herself to fail. I opened with the duchess on one of her darkest days, the death of her youngest child, and I wanted to end with the duchess, on a far happier day.

3

In addition, there were scenes I could not add to the individual books because they would have been spoilers, or they would have added too many pages, or because they weren't *about* any of the main couples. I wanted to revisit the characters from earlier books when they learned who would inherit the dukedom, and see how they were getting on a year or more after the end of their story. These scenes didn't fit in the context of any one book, but they add something to the overall series.

So here is the epilogue to the Desperately Seeking Duke series. I hope I've answered most of your questions here (no, I am not planning to write a book about Jack, but I'm thrilled so many people want more of him). Thank you, dear reader, for reading along, and I hope you've come to love this family as much as I do.

~Caroline

DESPERATELY SEEKING DUKE

CHAPTER 1
EDINBURGH

It was by all appearances an ordinary trial in the Court of Justiciary in Edinburgh.

At one table, the Lord Advocate, prosecutor for the Crown, leaned back in his chair, looking eminently satisfied. The case before the court looked very clear: a common fence from Glasgow, charged with receiving goods stolen from Edinburgh merchants over the last several months. The accused, Adam Fergusson, had been named by the admitted thieves; some of the stolen goods had been found in his home; and he looked the part, long-faced and pale with small dark eyes that darted around constantly.

Mr. Campbell, the Lord Advocate, had already presented the case against Fergusson. Every witness had been unequivocal. Campbell had been overheard telling his clerk they would have the man convicted by dinner.

Felix Duncan got to his feet and smoothed down his robe to present the case for the defense.

A very pretty young lady with a generous bosom was his first witness. She smiled, showing her dimples, at the clerk who guided her to the witness stand, and two of the judges sat up a little straighter.

"I am Magdalen Fergusson, sister of Adam Fergusson," she said, her voice clear and sweet in the crowded courtroom. "I have known him all my life and kept house for him these last three years in Paisley, neither of us being married.

"One day this January past, I was at home with him when some gentlemen came to call. One of them was an old friend of my brother's whom I had met before, Mr. Tom Browne." She paused, her chin trembling. "He was a very bad influence on Adam, tempting him into gambling and drinking and such. I never liked to see him come."

The Lord Advocate yawned. Tom Browne and Edward Stephens had been arrested as part of a ring of thieves terrorizing Edinburgh. Browne had turned on his fellow thieves in exchange for a King's Pardon, and Stephens had already been found guilty and sentenced to hang. The ringleader of the thieves, William Fletcher, would have suffered the same, had he not fled town and washed up dead in the River Clyde.

Felix gave Campbell a reproving glance. "Pray continue, Miss Fergusson."

She nodded solemnly. "Mr. Browne and the other fellows came to our house several times, always bringing parcels which they asked Adam to hold for them." She turned toward the judges imploringly. "My brother is a good and decent man, and he wanted no trouble! He acted only to help an old friend, but I always knew that Tom Browne to be a bad sort. *He* were the one who brought the others to our house, those thieves. Adam is guilty of nothing but excessive affection for an old friend, and of trusting too much in the word of a lying traitor."

Campbell rose. "What was in these parcels, Miss Fergusson?" So far it appeared she'd come to confirm her brother's guilt, and he flashed a vaguely impatient glance at Felix.

"Why, I've no idea." Miss Fergusson opened her big blue eyes wide, the picture of innocence. "None of them told me, sir, and Adam didn't look. That would be betraying a confidence, and Adam's an honest fellow."

Felix was impressed in spite of himself. This woman should be on the stage. Campbell sat down and bent over his papers.

"I advised Adam to have nothing to do with them, but then one of the gentlemen went out of his way to win my regard. He began to bring me gifts, sir, and I—" She stopped, her chin wobbling. "I was taken in by his cruel lies, Your Honors!"

One of the gentlemen of the jury stirred. "What nature of gifts?"

Magdalen Fergusson bit her plump, pink lip. A tear hung from her long eyelashes. "Three gold rings, and a pair of shoe buckles. Some bolts of silk. I had two of them made up into dresses."

"You claim your brother did not open the parcels these men left with him. Are you certain of that?" asked Felix.

"Of course Adam wouldn't," she exclaimed. "Mr. Hewitt's not a man to cross!"

A stir rippled through the courtroom. The Lord Advocate's head came up.

"Mr. Hewitt?" Felix furrowed his brow. "Do you not mean Edward Stephens, or William Fletcher?"

She shook her head. "No, sir. Mr. Liam Hewitt. He and Tom Browne were thick as thieves, and they were the men who brought those parcels to our home."

Mr. Campbell was on his feet again as whispers swept the courtroom. "How did you know it was Liam Hewitt?"

"Why, he gave me his name as such, and Mr. Browne called him by it. I will describe him. He is about twenty-six years old, moderately tall, with brown hair and light brown eyes but much darker eyebrows. And—" She blushed again. "He has a crescent-shaped scar upon his chest, here." She drew one hand down her throat to lay it on her left breast, capturing every man's eye.

Mr. Campbell seemed stunned speechless, or perhaps was simply mesmerized by the way she touched her breast.

"Miss Fergusson, do you mean to suggest Mr. Hewitt was involved in the recent burglaries in Edinburgh?" demanded one of the judges.

"Involved! Why, he planned them," she said, eyes wide and innocent. "He boasted of it to me, and he said we would be married so that I would never have to say a word against him in court."

The stir became a dull roar. Campbell shot an accusing glare at Felix, who kept his somber, slightly troubled expression in place.

"How do you know Hewitt planned the robberies?" demanded someone from the jury.

"He told me how he did it. He was very proud of it." Miss Fergusson turned a guileless gaze upon the judges. "He took the spare keys from the shops when no one was looking and made false keys from them. He's one of the best locksmiths in Mr. Fletcher's cabinetry shop, he said."

"Wait, wait!" Campbell howled. "Mr. Hewitt is not on trial!"

"Perhaps he should be," said Felix sotto voce.

The Lord Justice-Clerk held up his hands, scowling. "Miss Fergusson, confine your statement to this case."

She nodded. "As you wish, Your Lordship. I only thought you should know who broke into all those shops and stole all those things, because it's not right that Mr. Stephens will hang for them and Mr. Hewitt, who induced him to do it, is a free man, able to take up robbing and stealing again at any moment."

Pandemonium broke out. Spectators were shouting, the clerk of court was calling for order, half the gentlemen of the jury were on their feet, pointing and arguing, and the judges were huddled together in furious conference. The Lord Advocate gave Felix a withering look and leaned toward him. "I do not appreciate being ambushed, Mr. Duncan."

"I did try to speak to the Sheriff, but he refused to see me," returned Felix. "I suspect he will now."

Campbell snorted. "When did you approach him?"

"Yesterday." Felix held up one hand at the Lord Advocate's growl. "Miss Fergusson was hesitant to speak against a man not under arrest, and only decided she must when she saw the peril her brother was in."

"So this is a woman spurned?" Campbell eyed her. Magdalen Fergusson still stood in the witness box, looking like innocence betrayed.

"A woman deceived and abused, coming virtuously to the aid of justice," corrected Felix. "How do you think she knows what scar Hewitt has on his breast?"

Campbell sighed. "There'll be hell to pay over this. Deacon Fletcher was all but hanged in effigy for the crime, and now she's accused someone else entirely!"

Felix shrugged and began to organize his papers. The judges had withdrawn to discuss what to do, but this would not be sorted out in a brief conference. "Perhaps the Fletcher family will accept an apology from the Crown and sheriff. We'll call upon you tomorrow, to produce Miss Fergusson's proof of Hewitt's guilt." He paused, as if a thought had just struck him. "If I were you, Mr. Campbell, I'd suggest the sheriff keep an eye on him, to be certain he doesn't slip through your fingers. Cockburn seems to have trouble keeping track of people."

"Aye, aye," grumbled Campbell. His clerk was already plowing through the seething scrum of people toward Mr. Cockburn, the Sheriff-depute of Edinburgh.

The judges returned; court was dismissed. One judge, Lord Lindow, gave Felix a penetrating look from the bench. He bowed respectfully.

Beside Felix, his partner William Hunter shook his head. "Now I see why you took this case. You hardly ever argue criminal cases, but this one... no, this one *hopeless* case we must take, and drop everything to argue it."

Felix didn't look at him. They both knew very well Adam Fergusson was a longtime fence and petty thief, and his sister had been a willing and able accomplice. She had believed Hewitt's protestations of affection and intent to marry her, until she reached Edinburgh and tried to see him. Hewitt, it turned out, had another woman in Edinburgh who was pregnant with his child. Felix wondered if the scoundrel had lovers all over Scotland.

When Magdalen found that out, she'd flown into the sort of fury that made men cower in their boots, and vowed to see Hewitt punished for his crimes. She had the means to do it, too: she'd kept letters and gifts from him, including items stolen from Edinburgh merchants. And she was willing— eager—to show them to the court.

Felix grinned at his partner. "When have you seen this much excitement in court?"

Hunter had to laugh. "Never!"

A man forged through the crowd toward them, a triumphant look on his face. Michael Oliphant was the attorney Adam Fergusson had originally retained, until Magdalen arrived in Edinburgh for the trial two days ago and discovered her lover's betrayal. Oliphant wasn't stupid; the moment Magdalen came into his office, breathing fire over Hewitt's faithlessness and swearing she would see him hanged, he sent a man to Felix.

Deacon Fletcher, the supposed head of the thieving ring, had left behind a daughter Ilsa, who was now married to Felix's brother-in-law. Not only that, Ilsa was dear friends with Felix's wife Agnes. Ilsa refused to believe her father was a thief, and Agnes loyally supported her. When Oliphant's clerk showed up in his office offering a chance to clear Fletcher's name, Felix put off all his other clients and leapt on it.

"Brilliant!" Oliphant clapped his shoulder. "Half the people in the Tolbooth will be clamoring for you, after this."

Felix grinned. "You haven't won Fergusson's case yet."

"Oh, I daresay the Sheriff and the Lord Advocate will be willing to strike a deal now," said Oliphant easily.

"Jump to it, man." Felix glanced back at Magdalen, finally being helped from the witness box by a solicitous member of the jury. "She'll come for you next, if you don't."

As he turned to go, Felix glanced upward at the spectator gallery. A tall, spare man dressed all in black sat in the front row, his hands clasped on the head of his cane, as calm as everyone else was agitated. He tipped his head in salute.

Felix hid his surprise and returned the nod. His father had finally come to see him argue a case.

The tap on the door came ten minutes after she'd closed the shop. Louisa St. James bustled through the quiet salon to peek around the curtain.

She recognized the man outside, and hastily turned the key in the lock. Since they'd been robbed several months ago, she kept the doors securely bolted whenever she was alone in the shop, as she was now.

"Come in, sir," she said, opening the door.

Lord Lachlan Duncan stepped in, removing his hat. "Good evening, madam."

"Is aught amiss with Felix or Agnes?" she asked curiously. Her eldest daughter, Agnes, had married Lord Duncan's son, Felix, and moved into his rooms in Burnet's Close. They had finally located a house and were preparing to move; that was what brought Louisa back into the shop she'd handed over to her daughter two months previously. Agnes was busy packing, and Louisa was behind the familiar counter for a week.

"Nay, not at all." He turned the hat around in his hands. The judge was a lean man, as tall as his son, but far more somber. "I came to tell you he did well in his case today."

Louisa waited expectantly.

Lord Duncan cleared his throat. "He represented a man accused of receiving stolen property, goods stolen from a number of merchants in Edinburgh. A quantity of jewelry, some tea... some bolts of silk."

She went rigid. That silk had been stolen from *this* shop. The theft had terrified her; the thieves had shattered every glass cabinet and shredded several bolts of expensive cloth. She'd had nightmares about it for months, even after arrests had been made.

"I don't wish to alarm you," the judge hastened to say. His brilliant blue eyes scanned her face. "I only thought you might wish to know... The defendant's sister gave testimony about the men who brought the stolen goods to their home."

"Browne," said Louisa through stiff lips. "Stephens." She had to swallow. "And Deacon Fletcher."

"Aye, Browne and Stephens." The judge nodded. "Not Fletcher, though. Mr. Liam Hewitt."

It took a moment to register. Louisa blinked. "Not—not Deacon Fletcher?"

When Deacon Fletcher had been accused of being the mastermind of the thieves' ring, he'd fled—Ilsa had gone after him, and Andrew had gone after *her*, bringing suspicion down on all of them.

Which was rubbish, of course. Andrew had nothing to do with the robberies. Ilsa still proclaimed her father's innocence, but she'd given quite a bit of money to victims of the robberies. Louisa knew because Felix had handled it for Ilsa. It had seemed the entire ordeal was at a sad end.

But this... She pressed a hand to her throat. "What does that mean? Mr. Hewitt was also involved?"

Lord Duncan hesitated. "I believe," he said slowly, "that it means the deacon was wrongly accused. There was no established connection between Fletcher and either Browne or Stephens, but Hewitt was a well-known companion to both of them. Hewitt was a wright and locksmith in Fletcher's workshop, with the same skills the Deacon might have had. And I understand there is a nefarious connection between him and Fletcher as well, giving him a motive to cause harm to the Deacon's good name."

Louisa said nothing. Hewitt was Fletcher's natural son, but unacknowledged, and he'd harbored some resentment toward Ilsa because of it. Andrew had told her in strictest confidence, as a warning to avoid the man.

The judge cleared his throat. "In any event, the witness gave enough evidence to spur an inquiry into Mr. Hewitt's actions and connections to the robberies. Mr. Cockburn, the sheriff, will not like being made to look a fool. He will be thorough."

He didn't add "this time," but they both understood it.

She nodded. "Thank you for coming to warn me."

"I expect they will act with more discretion and honor now." Lord Duncan tilted his head, watching her closely. "You must tell me if they do not."

She mustered a smile. "I suppose they will want to speak to Andrew and Ilsa again?" She bit her lip. "Poor Ilsa, to have it all dragged up again when her father's dead and cannot know he was exonerated."

"One hopes the clearing of his name will offer her some solace."

Louisa nodded. On impulse she touched his sleeve. "Thank you, sir. It restores my faith in the good men of Edinburgh."

He seemed mesmerized by the sight of her hand on his arm. "Are you still planning to remove to London, Mrs. St. James?"

"Remove!" She gave a little laugh. "Nay. A visit only, next spring. My younger daughters are wild to see it, and now that Agnes has taken control of the shop, I confess that a holiday south has some appeal. But only for a few months," she ended with a smile. "I'm a Scotswoman, through and through."

He nodded. "Very good."

For a moment they stood in silence.

"May I walk you home?" he asked abruptly.

Louisa's brows went up. "Now?"

He wouldn't look at her. "If you are ready to leave, yes."

She folded her arms. "Why would you want to do that?"

Since his son had married her daughter, Louisa and the judge had become well acquainted. They liked many of the same books, although the judge rolled his eyes at the romantic novels Louisa and her daughters read and she had little interest in his legal tomes. They both liked good wine and a well-laid table, chamber music and walks in the heather. She had invited him to accompany her to botanical lectures, and he'd offered to teach her how to play golf—several times. Since he'd finally gone to a lecture, she supposed it was time for her to learn golf. He was intelligent, with a sharp, quick humor and a keen, practical sense of responsibility. She liked him very much.

His mouth thinned. "Do you not want me to?"

"I wish to know why you want to."

The judge put back his shoulders and faced her as gravely as he might have passed sentence from the bench. "I admire you, madam, very much. It would bring me great pleasure to offer you my arm this evening."

She pursed her lips. "And would you be coming in for a bite of dinner and a glass of wine when we get there?"

He blinked, frowned, then his brows went up. "If I were invited... Aye."

Louisa gave a short nod. "You're invited. Wait while I fetch my hat and cloak."

"Did Felix say aught to you about it?" he called as she hurried through the shop.

She waved one hand. All three of her daughters had been teasing her for some time now about the judge's attentions. Even Felix had mentioned it, saying he'd rarely seen his father in such good humor. "As if I can't tell when a man's interest is piqued without being told! I've been wondering for months if you would ask me something."

His face was set in a deep frown when she came back. He was so somber, so unlike her late husband. George had been a prankster, always jolly and amiable. Yet somehow, Louisa thought George would have liked the judge.

"Months," he said under his breath as she locked the door behind them. "I could have asked months ago?"

"Aye." She put her hand on his offered arm. "Pay more attention in future, my lord."

His sharp crack of laughter echoed off the stone buildings. "You may depend upon it, my dear, I shall."

Agnes was in the cramped sitting room, surrounded by packing crates, when Felix flung open the door, his arms spread wide in triumph. "Mrs. Duncan, I have done it."

She stood up from the open crate in front of her. "You did?" He nodded. "Really? Oh, Felix, Ilsa will be *so* happy!" She bounded over a stack of books waiting to be packed and threw her arms around him. "May I write to tell her?"

"If you wait until morning, you can surely send a newspaper with it." He clasped his hands behind her back.

"Tell me all about it," she said eagerly, pulling him down on the sofa with her. "Oh, I should have gone—I wanted to see—"

Felix told her, including every detail. He'd already told her about Magdalen Fergusson; Agnes had understood at once what the woman could do and she'd urged him to take the case, even before he could tell her he intended to. It turned out his wife had a mind for legal maneuvers.

He'd been in love with her before, but this absolutely dazzled him. If she hadn't been so dedicated to her silk shop, he would have begun to wonder if there weren't some way he could bring her on as a partner.

"So now what?" she demanded at the end of his story. "I *knew* I should have gone." She gave the nearest crate a half-hearted kick. "If only we weren't moving house tomorrow..."

"I expect the sheriff is now getting a warrant for Liam Hewitt. Miss Fergusson says she has proof."

She laughed. "Of course she does! I expect she kept his letters and every token he gave her." She glanced at the mess in the sitting room. "Not unlike you. Have you ever discarded anything?"

"Of course I have." He frowned in affront. "It only looks a great mess because it's all been taken out of the cupboards..."

Agnes nodded. "And the bookcases, and the desk, and that old trunk in your spare room. In fact..." She put one hand in the pocket of her dust-streaked apron. "Whilst you were out saving the city from thieves, I discovered something fascinating myself."

Felix went still, thinking hard, but he couldn't think of anything terrible she might have found. There were no miniatures of former lovers, no letters from another woman, no ribbon-bound locks of hair; he'd made certain anything remotely connected to other women was gone before his wedding day. His sitting room held nothing but the normal detritus of a bachelor gentleman.

Still...

"Oh?" he asked in a neutral voice. "Fascinating in a favorable way, I hope."

She gave him an appraising look. Very like a judge would give a witness on the stand before asking a portentous question. "That remains to be seen." She drew out a folded letter, addressed to him. "I do believe it will solve a small mystery that has vexed me for some time. Do you recognize this handwriting?"

Slowly Felix nodded. "Yes, Mr. Michael Oliphant wrote that."

"A friend of yours?"

His lips twitched. "You know he is. A fellow attorney."

"Indeed," she murmured, sounding exactly like the Lord Advocate. "Is he a good friend?"

"Moderately close, I would say."

She smiled. "He must be very fond of you, to do you such a favor."

Comprehension dawned. Long ago, in the first flush of his flirtation with her, he'd schemed to send her family tickets to the Assembly Rooms. He'd longed to dance with Agnes, but he knew the St. Jameses couldn't afford it, and her mother would have viewed the gift as wildly improper if he simply sent them with his compliments. So Felix had badgered every friend he had for an unused ticket and told them to sign them illegibly, so no one would never know.

It had nearly blown up in his face, when he and Agnes got too drunk to keep their hands off each other that night. But now that she was sitting here beside him, looking inclined to forgive him and perhaps even laugh about it, he decided to confess.

Felix closed his eyes and smiled ruefully. "I left it in the desk, didn't I?"

"Yes, you did. It was you!" she charged, waving the piece of paper in his face and bouncing onto her knees. "I was *certain* those tickets were from Ilsa!"

"I'm certain she wanted you to attend," he offered. "In spirit they were from her as well."

"Hmph." Agnes folded her arms, looking at him with narrow eyes, but a faint smile as well. "You might have told me."

"Told you!" He affected surprise. "And give away my entire wicked plan?"

"Wicked—?" She blushed, remembering. "That was not your plan. You told me so."

"No," he agreed, "my original plan was merely to dance with you, not drape you over my lap and put my hands inside your bodice and kiss you right here—"

She laughed as he began to re-enact the debauchery that had nearly ruined their romance before it began. "Why didn't you tell me?"

"You never asked," he murmured, his lips against her jaw.

"How was I supposed to suspect?" She let him urge her back against the arm of the sofa, swinging her legs over his lap all on her own.

Felix held up one finger. "You were not supposed to suspect. You were supposed to believe them sent from Heaven, a sign from the Almighty that you were meant to dance with a poor lawyer and fall madly in love with him..."

"How was I supposed to deduce something that fantastical?" She was still laughing at him.

He lifted one shoulder. "I don't know. I would have settled for simply being the closest man nearby when you decided you wanted to dance."

She looked at him, her blue eyes soft. "Did you really want to dance with me that desperately, that you persuaded your friends to give up their tickets?"

"I wanted to dance with you more than anything," he answered honestly.

She laughed again, and he trailed one finger down her throat.

"Thank goodness you did," she said softly. "For I do love you, sneaky fellow that you are." She put her arms around his neck and kissed him. "Thank you."

"My dear," he said as he tugged loose the ribbon on the front of her dress, "you are well worth four tickets to the Assembly Rooms. Perhaps as many as *eight* tickets."

"Felix Duncan," she began, only to laugh as he wiggled his brows and bent his head.

Then she pulled him closer, and kissed him back.

CHAPTER 2
STORMONT PALACE

Ilsa St. James set her feet and adjusted her grip, taking a slow, steady breath.

"Lean over a bit more," said her husband, watching from a few feet away.

She frowned, bent her knees a little more.

"No, *lean*," said Drew. "And turn a bit to the left."

Left was away from the hole. What was he about? She glanced up, frowning again, and caught his wicked smile. She realized the kerchief around her neck had come loose, exposing the top of her breasts. With an exclamation, she tore it off, wadded it up, and threw it at him. "Cheat!"

"Cheat!" He was laughing. "I'm only offering helpful advice..."

"You are trying to distract me, and I will not allow it." She pointed her golf club at him for emphasis. "Now, quiet, please, while I make this shot." She ignored him this time as she eyed the ground, then gently tapped her ball. It rolled five feet and dropped into the hole.

She stood, smiling in satisfaction, and propped the club

on her shoulder as she strolled over to Drew. "Your turn," she told him sweetly.

His gaze dipped to her bosom for a moment before he looked away. His ball was farther from the hole than hers had been, and up a gentle rise from it. He had the trickier shot by far.

They had a wager on the game, of course. She had given him the clubs as a wedding gift, since there was a course conveniently near Stormont Palace. It was only one of the many things they loved about the estate, and they'd barely been back to Edinburgh. Ilsa had even deeded her house in town to her Aunt Jean.

Now they played a round every few days, as long as the season would allow. Usually Drew won, but Ilsa was improving; today she was up by a stroke. If he made this, they would be tied.

She rested both hands on her club and gave a little wiggle of her shoulders. "Take your time," she said airily. "If you don't line it up just right, you'll go astray."

He looked at her, then at her breasts, about to spill over her bodice without the kerchief. Mouth tight, Drew turned his eyes back to his golf ball. "Quiet," he growled.

Ilsa strolled around to stand just behind the hole, in his line of vision. Again she leaned over, way over, as if studying the ground, her torso almost parallel to the ground.

Her husband made another growling sound.

"What?" She glanced up and blinked innocently. "It's a very challenging lie. I want to study your technique."

"After I make this shot," he said, his voice low and dangerously calm, "I'm coming over there to take off the rest of your dress and throw you in the river. And then I'm going to jump in after you and make love to you on yon sunny rock, out where all can see."

Without thinking, she looked toward the river. Drew hit his ball, and it rolled down the slope, picking up speed as it went, bumped over the hole, and kept going into the tall grass behind Ilsa, where Robert was helping himself to a bite to eat.

She gasped, then thrust both fists in the air. "I win! I win! I beat you, at last—" She broke off as he threw down his club and came at her, kilt swinging around his knees and a dangerous gleam in his eyes. "I won!" she cried one last time before grabbing her skirts and running. Robert gave an excited whinny in support.

Drew caught her within twenty yards, his arms around the waist, and lifted her, shrieking, off her feet. "There is nothing so attractive as a woman who can golf," he growled. He pressed his mouth to the side of her neck.

"And a woman who beats you at golf?" asked Ilsa breathlessly.

"Unspeakably arousing," he whispered back. His hands had wandered up her bodice and stroked her exposed breasts. All that leaning over and running had rendered her quite indecent, and now she didn't care.

Ilsa spun around in his embrace and gripped his face with both hands. "Prove it," she whispered. "I demand a victory prize."

Drew's gaze darted from side to side. The marshy course presented precious few sheltered spots, and despite his wicked words, Ilsa knew he wouldn't actually strip her naked where anyone might spy them. They had made love outdoors before, but now Drew was a respectable man of the community, a landowner, and anyone in Perth might come strolling over the rise with a bag of clubs on his arm...

"All right," said Drew, his eyes dark with desire. "In the taller grass over there. You'll have to be on top—keep watch for intruders—"

Ilsa gasped, trying not to laugh at the same time. "You expect me to ignore what you're doing and keep watch?"

"You won't ignore me," he murmured with a heated look. "But I'll be quick."

She gave in and laughed even as her insides quivered with anticipation.

A shout interrupted their negotiations. Drew started to duck out of sight, but Ilsa had seen the newcomer. "It's Bella," she said, yanking her kerchief from her husband's pocket and hurriedly tucking it back around her bodice.

He groaned. "Why?"

"I don't know, but she's spotted us, and you know she won't go home without speaking to us now." She waved an arm over her head.

Drew muttered a few more imprecations under his breath before turning and raising a hand at his sister's approach.

"Have I missed the game?" Bella demanded breathlessly as she drew near. "Are there still a few holes to play?"

"No," said Drew firmly. "What brings you all the way out here?"

Her face fell, but only a little. "A letter arrived for you." She dug into her cloak pocket. "By express messenger. I thought it might be... urgent." Face flushed, she held out a thick letter, the Carlyle seal stamped deep into the red wax.

. . .

Drew stared at the letter his sister held, his heart suddenly thundering in his ears. Slowly he put out a hand, glancing at his wife as he did so. Ilsa had gone pale, all the laughter fading from her face. A letter from Carlyle. It must be— It might be— But why else would they write to him? He communicated every other month with Mr. Edwards about estate matters. The last, mundane, letter from the attorney had arrived only a fortnight ago.

He took the letter, then abruptly released Ilsa and turned to walk a few steps away. He heard Bella inhale indignantly, and Ilsa's murmured word of restraint. His hands shook as he broke the seal and unfolded the letter.

It was from Edwards. It did not, as Drew had feared, announce the death of the duke.

He could barely comprehend what it *did* say.

He must have read it three times before Ilsa gave a little cry behind him. Drew spun around and saw that she too had a letter in her hands. "What?" he demanded.

"It's from Agnes," cried Bella, backing up. "It can't be terrible or she would have written to us, too!"

Drew started toward Ilsa, who was ashen-faced. "My father," she choked. Drew wrapped his arms around her on instinct, but she shrugged him off. "No, no," she said in a rush, her eyes beginning to glow. "'Tis good news! Agnes writes that Liam has been arrested for the robberies! My father has been cleared!" She burst into tears and clapped both hands over her face.

Drew glanced at Bella, who stared back, wide-eyed, as astonished as he was. "How?"

His weeping wife simply thrust the letter at him, and Drew read quickly. A client of Felix's... A witness who could

27

prove Liam Hewitt had led the gang of thieves who'd plagued Edinburgh for months... a courtroom uproar... the sheriff, embarrassed but defiant... Liam Hewitt in the Tolbooth jail.

Well. That was a dramatic turn. He re-read Agnes's words, brimming with excitement as she recounted how Felix had spotted the opportunity and leapt on it and masterfully guided the case through the court. There was quite a lot about Felix's brilliance, actually, which Drew mostly skipped. But there it was, in the enclosed slipping from a newspaper: the Lord Advocate had declared that, given the evidence against Mr. Hewitt, and the lack of evidence against Deacon Fletcher, in the Crown's view it was more likely than not that Deacon Fletcher had had nothing to do with the robberies.

Ilsa's father had never been charged, let alone tried and convicted. There was no pardon to be gained. But now Ilsa and her Aunt Jean could hold up their heads again in Edinburgh and cut down the whispers that had dogged them since Fletcher's disappearance.

"I have to write to him," Ilsa said suddenly.

"What?" Bella goggled at her. "Ilsa... Your father..."

Drew held up one hand to her and hastily pulled Ilsa aside. It was the first time she'd slipped, since that horrible day in Glasgow when Fletcher had told her he meant to disappear. "Go find Robert," he called over his shoulder at Bella. "He's chewed up several golf balls and my last shot went into the grass there." Bella scowled at him suspiciously but tramped off after the pony.

"Shh," he murmured to his wife. "You can certainly write to him." Ilsa had received one letter from her father, five months ago, posted from New York. Fletcher seemed to be taking to America, writing of bountiful opportunities for a man with a craft.

"I must—at once. How relieved he shall be—" She stopped short, hand on her lips.

Drew nodded in sympathy as understanding dawned on her face.

When accused of the thefts, Fletcher had chosen to escape to America instead of defend himself. He'd known Liam Hewitt was responsible... but Hewitt was Fletcher's natural son. He feared proving his own innocence would implicate Hewitt, whom Fletcher had trained as expertly as himself. Drew hardly thought Fletcher would be eager to come home and see his son hanged, after all he had sacrificed to prevent it.

Nor was Drew eager to see him come back. Not only had Fletcher's property been sold and the money donated to victims of the robberies, Fletcher had broken Ilsa's heart. He'd never told her he had a bastard son, and then he chose that son over her. Ilsa had recovered from that, mostly, but if her father came home, it would get stirred up again.

"Write to him," Drew said again. "Who knows where he may be now? Let him know the good news, but he should think very carefully before coming back to Scotland."

Ilsa's excitement had faded. She nodded, clutching the letter to her heart.

"It is good news," he added encouragingly. "I've long waited to see Liam Hewitt in the dock. I was certain it was only a matter of time, and here it is, sooner than I dared hope."

She smiled reluctantly. "I can be more forgiving here in Perth, fifty miles away from him."

Drew nodded. "Aye, but I enjoy the sweet scent of justice even from this distance."

They walked back to the green. Bella had collected the discarded clubs—Drew made a note that he still had a promise to keep to his wife, for her victory—and Robert was back, delicately picking chunks of apple from Bella's hand.

His sister looked between them. Drew made a slight grimace and she understood. "Was your letter also good news, Drew?" Bella asked cautiously.

He remembered; the paper was crumpled in his hand. "Yes," he said slowly. "The duke is well. The duchess is well. And I won't inherit the dukedom after all."

Bella's brows shot up. "What?"

Drew looked at his wife. Her cheeks were still damp and her eyes were puzzled. "They found another heir," he said. "A nearer one."

Ilsa's eyes widened. "Who?"

"Where?" demanded Bella at the same instant.

He looked at the letter again. "In America." Apparently America was where people routinely went to play dead. "It's the duke's brother, thought dead for thirty years. He was in America all this time. And he has two sons."

Ilsa's gaze darted to the left, in the direction of Stormont Palace. The duchess has deeded it to Drew last winter—as a wedding gift, Edwards had said, but Drew had understood it was to shift the burden of maintaining the property over to him, while keeping it in the family. Had he inherited the dukedom, as expected, Stormont Palace would have once again belonged to the Duke of Carlyle.

"They are not asking for the house back," he said.

Ilsa flushed. A moment later a wide smile bloomed on her mouth. "Let me understand... You are no longer the heir.

You have no further duty to Carlyle. You get to keep Stormont."

He nodded at each statement.

Ilsa flung herself at him. "That is wonderful, wonderful news!"

He held her close. Now that she'd said it aloud, he could admit the same thing: it *was* wonderful news. He'd been braced for a letter from Carlyle saying that the duke had died and he and Ilsa must leave Stormont, move south to Carlyle Castle, and take up the life of an English duke. He was prepared to do it, but he knew Ilsa dreaded the prospect.

Now they would never have to go.

Even more... Edwards wrote that he hoped any disappointment caused by this news would be tempered by the happy reunion of a family. The duchess was pleased beyond all expressing, the attorney wrote, and the duke had declared he meant to make annuities of the sums the duchess had promised Drew and his cousin Maximilian, and even to increase it. The Carlyle estate would allot each of them two thousand pounds a year for the rest of their lives.

Drew would have felt well compensated simply being released from his future obligations—he knew Stormont had been irrevocably granted, along with all its income—but he could put the annuity to good use, too. Bella and Winnie still needed dowries. Agnes had declared the shop was her dowry, and neither Felix nor Drew dared argue with her.

"Wait a moment," said Bella slowly. "*Wait one moment.* If you're not to be the duke... And you won't have a seat in Parliament... Are we still going to London? You promised me and Winnie a season!" She looked half anguished, half furious.

Drew put back his head and laughed and laughed, until

Ilsa joined in and Bella folded her arms crossly. "I am not joking!" she said through her teeth.

"Nor am I." Drew threw an arm around his sister's shoulders. "We can still go to London. But now, it will be entirely for your sake and Winnie's, aye? No estate business, only parties and shopping and dancing."

Bella's face cleared. "Oh! Then I agree with Ilsa. This is *wonderful* news."

As if in agreement, Robert shook his head and spat out what was left of Drew's leather golf ball.

W inifred St. James was brushing tiny burs out of Cyrus the cat's fur when her sister Bella came tearing into the room, out of breath and wild-eyed. Cyrus, who had been stretched on his back with all four feet in the air, twisted with a yowl and shot under the bed.

"Drew's not to be the duke," Bella blurted out. "He's never going to have Carlyle Castle, but he said we'll still go to London, and also Ilsa's father has been proved innocent and Ilsa wants to write to him, *did you know he was still alive?*"

Winnie stared. "What?"

Bella, breathing hard, paused. "Which part has amazed you more? Because I found all of it shocking and astonishing."

Winnie held up one hand. Bella, she thought, needed to begin acting more like a lady. She would have to, when they went to London. Winnie was determined to make a stunning debut, and a wild, rackety sister wouldn't help. "What about Drew and the duke?"

Bella inhaled. "A letter came for him, by special messenger. It looked important, so I took it out to the links where he and Ilsa were playing." Another lungful of air. "And it was from Carlyle Castle, as I knew it was because I recognized the seal, and when Drew opened it, it said they had found another heir." She paused to breathe again. "So that means Drew won't be the next duke, though he will get to keep this house, and he says we shall still go to London but I am *worried*."

Winnie jerked upright, seizing on the most vital point. "Not go to London!"

Bella's eyes slid sideways. "Well, he said we would..."

Winnie leapt to her feet, outrage burning in her heart. "Of course we shall! He promised! Even Mama is looking forward to it!"

Her sister waved both hands impatiently. "There was also a letter from Agnes, for Ilsa, and she said Felix had located proof that Ilsa's father was innocent."

"Well, that is good news," exclaimed Winnie, only slightly diverted from the thought of London. "What a comfort it must be to Ilsa."

Bella nodded, watching her closely. "Yes. It must. So much, Ilsa said she would write to her father to tell him."

Silence filled the room.

"He's dead," said Winnie.

"So thought I!" cried her sister. "But now I wonder..."

Winnie considered it for a moment, incredulous but also wondering. Was it possible? Would Ilsa have kept such a thing secret? From everyone?

Then she shook her head. "No," she declared. "They found his body. Ilsa must have wished it, or perhaps she writes him letters even though he's dead. Like the way Mrs. Finch used to speak to her husband after he died." Mrs. Finch had lived next door to them in Edinburgh for a while, and spoke to her James as if he were present in the next room, until her two daughters came from Glasgow and took her to live with them. Mama said it comforted Mrs. Finch to talk to him still.

Bella looked doubtful.

Winnie took her sister's arms. "Bella. Remember how upset Ilsa was? It was heartbreaking, the way her father disappeared, and then her efforts to find him with Drew failed. I think we should leave her this bit of grieving. If you hound her about it and she falls into a melancholy, Drew will be furious. Ilsa doesn't deserve it. Also, if Drew is annoyed enough, he might put off our season in London, and if you cause that, I will never, *ever* forgive you."

Her sister twisted away and scooped up Cyrus, who had ventured from beneath the bed. "Perhaps you're right. I don't want to cause Ilsa more sorrow."

"So." Winnie sat at her dressing table. "Drew's not to be the duke? Has the Carlyle branch cut us off again?"

Bella made a face. "I don't think so." That meant she didn't know.

"We ought to find out," said Winnie thoughtfully. "When we go to London, we should know if we can mention the connection."

Cyrus wriggled, and Bella let him jump down. He loped across the room and settled on the sill of the open window, his tail swishing gently. "Why does it matter?"

Winnie sighed patiently. Bella was looking forward to the menagerie at the Tower, Vauxhall Gardens, the theaters. She had expressed no interest in gentlemen, except as dancing partners and interesting people to talk to. Winnie, on the other hand, was very interested in gentlemen. Most of the eligible men in Edinburgh had flirted with her at one moment or another, especially since Drew's brush with the dukedom, but she hadn't really liked any of them.

She was hoping for much more in London, even if it meant a life in England, if she married an Englishman. She hoped for someone from the north of England, who wouldn't mind coming to visit her family from time to time, but Winnie was determined to find her hero. Someone who would look at her the way her besotted brother gazed at Ilsa, fascinated and charmed and a little bit dazed, willing to make a fool of himself to coax her into some bit of naughty fun. Someone who cared about her thoughts and valued her opinion on literally everything, as Felix did for Agnes. Someone who could make her as lovestruck as her sister. Agnes, the most unsentimental of the sisters, wrote to them about her husband's musical ability—even though he had none—and his brilliant mind—which was real, but made for very dull reading.

No, London was where Winnie's hopes were pinned. If she were related to a duke and everyone knew it, she would be even more eligible, with more gentlemen interested in making her acquaintance.

"I only wondered," she said in reply to her sister. Bella wouldn't understand.

Bella sprawled in a chair. "If you marry someone in London, we'll never see you again."

She scoffed. "Only if you and Mama disown me! You'd be able to come to London any time you wanted, and stay with me. And of course I would visit Edinburgh, as long as Mama and Agnes are there, and Perth, as long as Drew and Ilsa are here." She glanced around the room as she spoke. She did like this house, very much. Drew had bought a much nicer house in Edinburgh for their mother, but Winnie adored Stormont.

"That's true," said Bella, perking up. "And if you marry some soft-chinned Englishman, I'd have Cyrus all to myself —" She ducked as Winnie threw a pillow at her. "You're very intent on this season, Winnie. What if London is terrible and you despise it?"

"I refuse to consider that possibility. It will be wonderful," she said firmly. "And you know what? I believe you will enjoy it, too."

CHAPTER 3

PERUSIA POTTERIES

Bianca hurried up the stairs to her father's office and knocked. "Papa? I'm sorry I'm late."

The door flew open. "Hush," he whispered harshly. "Must you be so loud?"

Bianca bit her lip to keep from laughing, but kept obediently silent as her father waved her into the room. All the windows behind his desk were tightly closed, and he'd even hung a thick curtain in front of them to muffle the noise of the workshops below. That made it warm and dim in the office, but there was no danger of stumbling. Papa had removed all of the shelves to make space for one new piece of furniture.

A cradle.

"I've come to feed him," Bianca whispered as she tiptoed behind her father.

"He's still asleep!" He eased into a chair and leaned forward to gaze proudly on his sleeping grandson, named for him. "Isn't he handsome when he sleeps?"

Bianca smiled. "He's beautiful." She stroked her son's wispy dark hair, almost long enough to curl now, like his father's.

Samual growled in his throat. "Don't wake him!"

She ignored him and gathered the sleeping baby into her arms. "He must eat," she said softly but firmly as she settled herself on the small sofa. "And I cannot wait around all day for him to wake. I'm expecting a fresh batch of tiles later."

Her father harrumphed. "The ebony glaze?"

"Yes." She tickled baby Sam's chin and he yawned, his pink mouth opening like a baby bird's. His eyes remained closed.

"How does it look?"

Bianca looked up. She and her father had disagreed—strenuously—about her return to the workshops after the baby's birth. Samuel thought she should not; Bianca was about to tear out her hair, being away from her workbench and the bustle of the factory and the company of other people. Poplar House was far enough away that she felt marooned and lonely with only an infant for company all day. Cathy came to visit for a while, but now her sister was also expecting a child, and unlike Bianca, whose good health had persisted for her entire pregnancy, Cathy was sick every morning and spent her days lying on the vicarage sofa with a large ceramic pot clutched in her arms.

Samuel was pleased beyond bearing to have one grandson and another on the way. But if he thought a baby would change Bianca's interest in her work, he'd been sadly mistaken.

"It's coming along beautifully," she told him. "I've got the color deep enough, and as soon as I figure out why some samples come back with a blue tinge, we'll be ready for full piece trials."

He was silent for a moment. "Excellent work," he finally said.

Bianca ducked her chin and grinned. She knew he was keenly interested in the new black glaze she'd been working on, despite all his muttering about motherhood. Her scarlet glaze had proved to be one of their best selling colors, and the factory had orders for ruby dinnerware to keep them busy for months. Even Max was surprised by how popular it was proving. But the deep dark ebony glaze would made extremely dramatic pieces, particularly with scenes of ancient Greece or Rome painted on top.

Another tap sounded at the door, almost as it swung open. "Your pardon, sir, is Bianca here?"

"Hush!" snarled Samuel again.

Max caught sight of her, cradling their son, and smiled. Helplessly Bianca returned it. She loved him more than ever. He had been the one who told Samuel in no uncertain terms that Bianca would return to her workshop when she wished to, and neither of them was going to tell her nay.

He'd also offered to put the cradle in Samuel's office, so the baby could be near Bianca but removed from the din and dirt of the factory, knowing the chance to watch his grandchild would appease his irritation at his daughter. Bianca had been struck breathless by the brilliance of this maneuver. Her father hadn't said another word of argument; in fact, he began asking when she would return.

Now Max slipped quietly into the room and came to sit beside her. He put the tip of his finger into his son's palm, and Sam clutched it in his sleep. "Not hungry yet, eh, my little man?" he murmured.

"He must be growing," Bianca whispered. "The midwife says he will sleep longer as he gets older."

"Would that it were at night," her husband shot back. "But I suppose now is also a good time. I've just had an unexpected visitor—"

"Go outside to discuss it," hissed Samuel. "This child is sleeping!"

Max gave Bianca an amused look. "If you insist," he said somberly, then took the baby from Bianca and placed the boy tenderly into an astonished Samuel's arms. "I need her for several minutes, so if you wake him, he'll have to cry," he said softly. "I suggest you don't move." He slipped his finger from the baby's grasp, letting it close around a button of Samuel's coat. The older man went still, transfixed by the tiny fingers on his button.

Max took Bianca's hand and pulled her to her feet. "Thank you, Samuel, I am deeply grateful." And he tugged her out the door before his father-in-law could protest.

He kept going until they were out of the building, in the courtyard of the factory. Bianca laughed and wound her arms around his neck. "You have raised my expectations beyond reason!"

He laughed and wiggled his brows. "Perhaps I schemed to get you alone, my love..."

She glanced at the throngs of people hurrying about their business all around them, some of whom still found time to cast an amused eye on the pair of them. By now they must have scandalized everyone in Marslip, from the way they were running Perusia together to the way they embraced in public.

In fact, she was strongly tempted to kiss her her husband

right in front of everyone. "We could hurry home," she said breathlessly. "Or down to Perusia Hall, no one will be there now..."

He paused, his eyes darkening. He was thinking about it. The baby did not sleep as well at night as he did during the day, and they didn't have nearly as much time alone together as they'd once enjoyed. "Alas, our visitor is waiting. Tomorrow," he promised. "Tomorrow we'll bring Sam here and leave him with your father, and *then* sneak back home together..." He gave her a slight smile, full of wicked promise. "I'll want a few hours at least, when I get you all to myself."

She laughed, and let him tuck her arm around his. "Who is the visitor?" she asked as they began a brisk walk through the factory yard.

"I think you'll be very interested to meet him. He's from Carlyle Castle."

M ax had been in one of the sculpting rooms, discussing the newest dishes for Fortuna ware with the modelers, when Ned found him.

"There's a gentleman to see you," said the factory manager. "I left him outside your office."

Max's brows went up in surprise. "Did he give a name?"

For answer Ned handed him a letter. Max's heart almost stopped at the sight of the handwriting. It was from Roger Edwards, the Carlyle solicitor.

"He said to give you that as his introduction," said Ned. He paused as Max stared at the letter. "Shall I send him away?"

Max jerked. "One moment." He walked out of the room,

around the corner, and down the ramp toward the canal. No barge was being loaded or unloaded at the moment, so the ramp was nearly deserted. He broke the seal and read Mr. Edwards's letter.

For a moment he stared, then he spun on one heel and strode back to where Ned lingered, talking about cricket with Bobby, who was up to his elbows in raw clay. "He's waiting by my office?" he asked.

Ned nodded. "He seemed curious about the place and asked for a tour, but I bid him wait."

Max nodded once. "Good. Thank you." He turned and hurried through the factory, taking the stairs two at a time.

His office was near the factory floor. It was loud and clay dust was everywhere, but he liked being closer to the workers. There was also no other space for it, as the production of Fortuna ware had crowded the factory to bursting. There were plans underway to expand the building.

The fellow waiting outside his office was a young man, not as tall as Max but brawny, brown-haired with dark eyes. He turned at Max's approach and bowed. "Mr. St. James?" he asked, his voice inflected with French.

"Yes. Come in, Mr. Montclair."

Max closed the door behind them, then couldn't hold back another moment. "Is it true? What Edwards wrote? Another heir?"

Montclair smiled. "It is incredible, no? But yes, it is true."

He began to explain why he'd come, but after a few minutes Max stopped him. "I beg your pardon," he said, his hand trembling the slightest bit. "May I fetch my wife? This concerns her as well."

Mr. Montclair sat back in his chair and grinned. "You

sound like my brother! By all means, fetch Madame St. James."

Max all but ran, finding her in her father's office cradling their four-month-old son. As always, the scene made his heart jump a little; today it squeezed so hard he couldn't speak for a moment. All this—his ownership stake in Perusia, his position in the business, his wife, his son, even his Aunt Greta's safety—he owed to Carlyle Castle, and the starchy duchess who'd looked down her nose at him.

It wasn't the first time he'd registered that thought, but somehow, today, it struck him with renewed force.

He handed off the baby to Samuel and hurried his wife outside. When he told her he had a visitor from Carlyle Castle, she stopped in her tracks.

"What? Please don't say something has happened to the captain!" Before he could reply she clapped one hand to her mouth. "Merciful heavens, has the duke—?" Her voice fell to a whisper.

"The duke is well." Max paused. "Very well. It turns out... Bianca, his younger brother survived."

Max had never once thought he would inherit Carlyle, but Bianca had worried over it. She'd become friendly with Miss Kirkpatrick, the duchess's ward, but she'd hated the castle and its distance from Perusia. He could tell his efforts to reassure her hadn't entirely worked, especially after his cousin the captain had gone missing for a few months. *He disappeared once, he could do it again,* she would say grimly.

She blinked at his statement. "The vicar? How is that possible? Didn't they bury him themselves? We saw the crypt."

"Not that brother," said Max. "The one who went off to

America and disappeared thirty years ago. He's alive, with two sons."

That should put him entirely clear of the dukedom, and end Bianca's worries.

She goggled at him. *"What?"*

Max spread his hands, beginning to grin. "I don't entirely understand how—something about a steward—but this brother's come home, alive and well. The captain and I are effectively supplanted from the succession."

"Are they certain it's the right man?" She was nibbling her lip, as she did when thinking hard.

Max took the letter from his pocket and offered it to her. "Mr. Edwards says it has been proven beyond a doubt."

She bent her head over the letter. "He doesn't explain why this brother disappeared," she murmured. "He doesn't explain why he came back now. He doesn't explain how anyone knew him. Max, what if he's not the real brother? Thirty years!"

It was his turn to blink, then he began to laugh. "All this time, I thought you wanted to be free of the possibility—"

"I did," she protested, her face pink. "I do!"

Still laughing, he cupped her cheek in one hand. "Whether he's the real man or an imposter, Edwards says the duchess is absolutely persuaded. I can only wonder what sort of proof it took to convince her, but it's done."

Her expression eased. "Yes, it must have been virtually an act of God to persuade her."

"Must have been," said Max wryly. Edwards also mentioned in the letter that the duke was making his allowance an annuity of two thousand pounds a year. Since the duchess had not hidden her certainty that Max would waste every farthing she gave him, all those months ago, this constituted iron proof to Max's mind that the duchess believed in this lost heir.

She studied the letter again. "Thank you for coming to tell me the good news, not only for you and me but for little Sam."

"Come with me to speak to him," he said when she started to turn back toward her father's office, where the baby was hopefully still asleep in his grandfather's arms. "The visitor from Carlyle."

"What more can he have to say?" She took his arm and walked with him. "It can't possibly be better than this!"

That was his Bianca: quick-thinking and practical. Max laughed, and they went inside.

For himself, this news made no difference. He'd breathed a sigh of relief when the captain had turned up again, alive and dutifully married, but no more than that. He'd already got more out of Carlyle than he'd ever expected to get. For all his wariness of the duchess, he had developed some respect for her, and her ward, Miss Kirkpatrick, was a delightful lady. He had even come to enjoy being able to rely a bit on his name. In his younger years, the connection had never brought him anything but bitterness. He'd lost his temper more than once when someone carelessly suggested he just appeal to his cousin the duke for funds when he was penniless. He had nursed more than a bit of grudge against the Carlyle St. Jameses, not knowing anything of them.

Now, though, he didn't hesitate to say *yes* when someone asked if he were a Carlyle relation. In some way, Max felt part of the family.

How odd, that he had gone from having no family at all to having two.

Mr. Montclair was in the doorway, neck craned to one

side as he peered down the corridor toward the main workshop. He straightened at their approach. Max introduced them, and all three went inside the office.

"For Madame St. James's sake, I will begin at the beginning, if I may." He paused expectantly, and Max nodded. "I am Jack Montclair. My father is Lord William St. James, younger brother to His Grace the Duke of Carlyle."

"How is that possible?" asked Bianca almost before the fellow finished speaking. "Forgive me, sir, but *how is this possible?*"

Mr. Montclair—Mr. St. James?—laughed. "I hardly believe it myself!" He paused, thinking. "All I ever knew was that my father had been a fur trader in the American wilderness before he met my mother in Quebec. My parents moved to Boston when I was an infant, and my brother, sister, and I grew up there." He paused again, as if he were trying to remember the details. "My brother Will knew more than I about our father's heritage, and he was eaten alive by curiosity about it. When we came to England on business, Will went to Carlyle, under disguise, to learn more. I understand that he... betrayed himself to Miss Kirkpatrick." The man was smirking, thought Max.

"Did Philippa—?" Bianca stopped herself. "My apologies, please continue."

Mr. Montclair smiled. "No, no, of course you have questions. She asked me to tell you that she is writing a long letter and will explain everything in great detail, if you will be patient and understanding. There is a tremendous tumult at the castle right now, you see."

"No doubt! I will eagerly await her letter."

Mr. Montclair leaned forward, now openly grinning. "She married my lunatic brother."

Max's brows went up and Bianca's mouth dropped open, though not a word came out.

Montclair was pleased with himself. "Forgive me," he said, opening his palms in a gesture of innocence. "I have been assaulted on all sides by shocking news for the last month. I could not resist making the surprise myself this time."

For a moment Bianca still stared. Then she choked, and then she began laughing, gripping Max's wrist.

"So, to business." Montclair was still smiling. "In America, my father and I run a shipping company." He made a face, but it looked more like delight than annoyance. "Now that my brother has fled our partnership to administer the castle, I am our premier agent in London. I came to England to form partnerships with merchants, to ship their goods to America, where there is an eager market for English luxuries, in exchange for materials from America. While at the castle I saw the tea service you presented to Her Grace the duchess." He glanced from her to Max and back again. "I understand you created the ruby glaze, Madame?"

Bianca nodded.

He smiled. "It is exquisite! That is exactly the luxury we desire to ship. I am here to propose a partnership, to bring Perusia wares to America."

Now it was Max's turn to be shocked speechless. He felt turned to stone for a moment even as his mind began to race through possibilities, as if a curtain were parting before him on a broad vista of wholly unexpected opportunities. An untapped market of pent-up demand in New York, Boston, Philadelphia. The rich soils and clays of America, at his fingertips. Good Lord. They had just taken a lease for a showroom in Liverpool, and he'd hoped to expand to Birmingham in a year, but now he could reach all the way across the Atlantic.

Could they even produce that much? The expansion plans would need to be expanded, and he'd have to poach more of Tom Mannox's workers—which, it must be admitted, would give him a visceral thrill. The redware vase still resided in Samuel's office after a second Perusia cricket victory.

Bianca looked at him, her eyes brimming with questions. Max caught his breath, gazing back. She knew him better than anyone else in the world, but she also knew this factory as well as he did. She would know if they could do it, or not. If she agreed...

B ianca could see it in his face: he wanted to do it. Oh, how he wanted it. He'd always had lofty aspirations and fantastic dreams.

Her father would object. They were running full speed already. The new factory wing being built was to accommodate Fortuna wares, not more Perusia pottery. The American market was nebulous, and so far away. It was pure speculation. Bianca knew those were valid points—just as she knew Max would forge through them all.

After all, he'd been right, time after time: about his ability, about Fortuna ware, about London and Liverpool, about how perfect they were for each other. Bianca had once thought their marriage was a tragedy of Shakespearean dimensions, but now recognized it as the best thing that had ever happened to her. To both of them.

Yet still he sat there, taut and waiting for her opinion. As he always did. *Will you trust me?* he'd once asked. She did. Always would.

"Let's do it," she whispered, and Max grinned, fierce and proud.

"Yes, Mr. Montclair," he said to the visitor. "We would be very pleased to discuss that sort of partnership."

K it Lawrence found his wife in the garden behind Poplar House, humming as she darned a pair of stockings. "Good day to you, Mr. Lawrence," said Jennie gaily.

"And to you, Mrs. Lawrence," he returned. He sat next to her on the bench. It was sunny out, and warm here behind the brick wall of the kitchen. The air smelled of fresh herbs and the last flowers of summer, fading away. "I've been down to the factory on an errand. I saw Mr. St. James there."

"Oh?" She bit off her thread.

Kit nodded. "He offered me a new position."

Jennie's scissors rattled on the bench as she shot to her feet. "What?"

He folded his arms and leaned back, closing his eyes against the sun. "Mm-hm."

His wife smacked him on the arm. "Kit! What position? Would we have to leave Persusia? What about Mrs. St. James?"

He squinted up at her. "Which am I meant to answer first?"

She put her hands on her hips and gave him The Look.

Kit grinned. "As his agent. Or secretary. Perhaps both."

"Doing what?"

"Helping run the showrooms and factories."

She caught the word at once. "Factories! How many?"

He shrugged. "Don't know. But he said there might be more than the one extra workshop already planned."

"That sounds like a great lot of work..."

He grinned. "It does. And vastly more interesting than polishing boots. I hope I'm up to it."

"He couldn't choose anyone better than you," declared his wife loyally. "Of course you're up to it! Well—that is—if you *want* to do it..."

Kit took a deep breath. "I do," he said quietly. He already managed most of Mr. St. James's correspondence, and spent several hours a day at the factory. He'd learned a great deal about the pottery business, and St. James had said it would be more of that—*much* more. He might be sent on business as Mr. St. James's agent to Birmingham and Liverpool, even to London.

With this promotion, Kit would no longer be a servant but a professional man. Oh yes, he wanted to do it.

"And we'll still be here?" She frowned. "But if you're at the factory all day, he'll need a new valet. Who—?"

"Yes, he'll need a new man. But Jennie—" He caught her hand. "It's substantially higher wages."

Her dark eyes rounded. "How much?"

Kit told her.

Jennie gave a little scream, then clapped her hands to her mouth. "With that much—"

He nodded. "And Mr. St. James said we'd have one of the new cottages being built near the birch grove. One of the larger ones."

There had long been cottages and boarding houses for Perusia workers. Mr. Tate's father had built some, and Mr. Tate had built more. Thanks to Mr. St. James's plans to create a new pottery line, they needed more workers, and were building more cottages.

Jennie inhaled raggedly. "But Kit—what about me?"

He tilted his head, taking hold of her hands. "It would be a long walk to remain in Mrs. St. James's service whilst living in the grove. I expect you'd have to leave her."

He knew she would be torn about that, but Jennie wanted to have a baby. Kit was all in favor, but it was difficult to have a child and remain in service as a lady's maid. With a house of their own and those higher wages, though... They could have a family.

She bit her lip. "But... What would I do?"

He glanced up at her. "What would you like to do?"

He knew, of course. She'd confided in him that her favorite part of her work was the clothing. Ever since their London trip, she'd begun making more and more of Mrs. St. James's clothing, and she had quite a hand for it. She pored over fashion magazines from London, and she was the one who urged her lady to try new styles. She remade old gowns and when they were good for little but fabric, she cut them into waistcoats for Mr. St. James. Kit had once heard Mr. St. James make a naughty joke about the pleasure of wearing his wife's skirts around his neck.

"There's no dressmaker in Marslip," he remarked. "All the women have to send to Stoke for cloth and designs. I expect someone who set up shop here, with fabrics and pattern books and taking commissions, would do well."

Jennie sat beside him with a swirl of skirts. "Do you really think I could?" she asked breathlessly.

He grinned. "If you want to, of course you could. The question is, *do* you want to?"

She hesitated.

He leaned forward and touched his forehead to hers. "Either way, I believe in you. You're talented enough, and you're clever enough. So think about it, aye?"

Her eyes sparkled with love. "Only you would encourage me in such madness, Kit Lawrence."

He kissed her. "And I look forward to doing it for many, many more happy years."

CHAPTER 4
CARLYLE CASTLE

R oger Edwards took a fortifying breath and looked at the gathering before him. Mr. Heywood, the butler, had summoned the entire household of Carlyle Castle so everyone could hear it at the same time. Edwards knew rumors had been flying for weeks now, and it was time to confirm them.

And, he must admit, he only wanted to do this once.

"Thank you all for your attention," he began. "I expect there have been some rumors, and His Grace asked me to address them."

A stir rippled through the household. No one could remember an assembly like this—because it had never happened.

"By now you must all know Mr. Montclair, who has been managing the estate," Edwards went on. "It has come to light that he has a... connection to the St. James family."

Now the stir was louder. Someone in the back whispered loudly, "I *told* you he weren't a proper steward!"

"There is no other way to put this," Edwards said. "It turns out Lord William St. James, His Grace's younger brother, did not die as everyone believed."

Now it was no longer whispers but a loud buzz of conversation.

"Lord William has been alive and well in America these thirty years." Edwards paused. "Mr. Montclair is his son."

"What?" burst out Heywood, the staid and reserved butler.

Mrs. Potter lurched upright and took two steps forward. "Mr. Edwards, are you saying...?"

He nodded gravely. "I am, madam. Lord William has returned home. Everyone, including Her Grace, is absolutely persuaded of his identity."

The hall erupted. Edwards kept one eye on Charles Amis, the duke's personal valet. He was staring at Edwards, eyes round and mouth clamped shut, even as his wife, the pastry cook, tugged at his arm. Edwards had wondered if Mr. Amis suspected something about the steward. He knew the two had become friends.

"What about the captain?" someone called out tentatively. "And Mr. St. James?"

"They remain heirs, but they have been supplanted. Lord William has two sons"—louder pandemonium—"and a daughter. They will be traveling here from London in a few days."

He let the tumult carry on for a few minutes. Montclair had made an impression on everyone from the laundry maids to the duke himself. Edwards did not think this news was disappointing to many.

"This means there will be guests at the castle," he said, raising his voice. "Her Grace would like Lord William and his family to see the castle at its best. In time, there will also be a fête." He paused. "I should say, there will be *two*. One for the parish, to present Lord William and his family, and one for all of you, at Miss Kirkpatrick's—that is, the new Mrs. Montclair's request."

As the hall erupted once more, Edwards made his way to the Amises. The valet gave him a long, hard look.

"Did you suspect, Mr. Amis?" Edwards asked him. He was been burning to ask this question for weeks now, wondering if the valet had seen what he himself had not.

The Black man shook his head emphatically. "Never."

His wife crossed her arms. "You said he wasn't like any steward you'd ever met, Charles."

"He isn't," he replied. "I did not suspect *this* was the reason."

Edwards looked between them. "He asked me specifically to speak to both of you, and convey his regret for any dismay you may feel at his deceptions."

"Dismay!" Maria Amis laughed in disbelief. "He'll be lord and master of this estate and he cares what we think?"

Edwards bowed his head. "He does." Montclair had been anxious about this; he'd wanted to tell the Amises before the family left for London, but Edwards had persuaded him to wait. He was still sorting out what needed to be done to have Lord William restored to his position as the duke's heir, and had guarded against the possibility it wasn't true, up until the very last moment, just in case.

He had not been foolish enough to say that to the duchess, obviously.

Mr. Amis nodded slowly. "I believe he would." He glanced at his wife. "I hope you have a great deal more cherry preserves, my dear. I suspect tarts will be very much in demand at both of these fêtes."

"No doubt," said Edwards dryly.

"Well!" Mrs. Amis shook her head again. "Of all things. The steward is heir to our duke!"

Mr. Amis began to chuckle. "What's that?" demanded his wife. He only laughed harder, until he was wiping his eyes and Roger Edwards was just as impatient as Maria Amis to know what was so amusing.

"And to think," gasped the valet, his shoulders shaking, "I once teased Montclair about waiting for a rich uncle to leave him an estate and fortune! Never in my life did I suspect that uncle would be the Duke of Carlyle."

An hour later Roger Edwards made his way to his office in the castle, his mood expansive. His time in London had been incredibly busy, but worthwhile. Consultations with a number of attorneys and ministers had established what he needed to do to restore Lord William's right to Carlyle, but assured him it could be done. *Would* be done.

In consequence he'd hardly got anything else done in town. His clerk had sent a parcel of documents and letters, and Edwards opened it, intending only a brief perusal. The duchess, her mood even better than his, had urged him to take a holiday for himself after the last few frantic weeks. He wasn't entirely certain she meant it, but it was the first time *she* had suggested he take a holiday, so he probably ought to seize the chance.

It had occurred to him that he might make a visit to Kittleston. His elderly father still lived there... as did Emily Calvert. She was a lovely woman, charming and sweet-natured, and they'd become prolific correspondents in recent months, about the school and other projects in town that she had carried on in Lord Stephen's memory and which the duchess still sponsored.

But he suspected Miss Calvert's heart wasn't as broken as it had once been, and he found that... intriguing.

The clerk's report was brief, listing the letters that had arrived, calling his attention to a particular one. Edwards went still, jerked out of his thoughts of Emily Calvert, at the sight of it.

He dropped the clerk's list and dug through the packet until he found the letter in question, stained and creased from long travel. It had come all the way from Philadelphia, from the agent he had sent looking for Lord Thomas St. James first in France, then in America.

He tore it open it and skimmed the first page—reporting that Lord Thomas and his family had been traced to Philadelphia, just before a smallpox outbreak had swept the city, killing hundreds—before he stopped.

Because... what did it matter? Nothing.

It did not matter.

It didn't matter whether Lord Thomas had survived the smallpox and fathered ten more sons, or if he and his entire family had perished. A month ago, Lord Thomas would have instantly become the closest heir presumptive, sending all sorts of tremors through the castle and the succession... but now, he was fourth in line and Edwards knew the duchess wouldn't be interested in spending another farthing on him.

Edwards didn't wish the man ill, but he was enormously relieved that he no longer had to look for Lord Thomas. *Fare thee well, sir,* he thought to the absent Frenchman.

Whistling, he tossed the letter, still mostly unread, into a drawer of his desk along with all the others, locked it, and left the office. He needed to pack his things for Kittleston.

T he reunion in London had gone far better than Will expected.

His sister, like his brother, had simply marveled at everything connected to Carlyle. Philippa was warm and enthusiastic. The duchess treated them all warmly, but gingerly, as if she feared saying the wrong thing and causing another rupture. Will had no idea what his mother thought, though, and his father had been cordial but reserved—utterly unlike himself. Several days after their arrival, on the verge of departing for Carlyle, he was still braced for... something. Neither of his parents would hold their tongues forever.

They left London in a caravan of carriages and riders. The duchess had a retinue, and everyone had tacitly agreed that sharing cramped carriages for two or three days was out of the question. One carriage carried the duchess, her maid, and Philippa, another carried more servants, and a third was for Will's mother and sister. Will, Jack, and their father all opted to ride, and the luggage trundled along behind in a wagon. For most of the trip, conversation was sporadic and inconsequential, as befitted a long journey, but three miles from the castle, Will's father suddenly peeled away and rode ahead.

Will, riding beside the duchess's carriage, glanced at Philippa. She leaned out the window and saw his father disappearing down the road, and her lips parted in dismay. "What is it?" asked the duchess anxiously.

"I'll find out," he promised, and urged Gringolet on

before the duchess could recover and pelt him with questions.

He still couldn't think of her as his grandmother, and he thought it would take her a long while to overcome her view of him as an impudent employee. She was far kinder to Jack and Sophie, and almost delicate with his parents, but her eyes still flashed fire at him from time to time. Philippa told him he must be patient. Will found that easier if he kept some distance.

As he rode past the next carriage, his sister's head and shoulders emerged from the window. "Où va-t-il?"

"Je ne sais pas," he replied, and nudged Gringolet into a canter.

He caught up where the road made its turn into the approach to the castle. The land dipped below them, then rose up again beneath the ancient walls. In the afternoon sun, the stone had a silvery quality. The gardens were still bright with the last of the summer greenery, the leaves on the towering oak tree just beginning to shift from green to orange.

His father sat motionless on his horse, the reins lax in his hand, staring at the castle. Will wondered what he must be thinking, after so many years away. Was it familiar? Was it dear? Was it dreaded? Was he regretting coming back?

With a clatter of hooves, Jack pulled his horse up. Jack had been insulted at being left in ignorance, and had developed an annoying habit of prying into everyone's business. "What?" he demanded breathlessly. "Why were we charging ahead?"

Will tipped his head toward the view.

Jack raised his brows, uncomprehending. "What about it?"

"Until this moment," said Pa softly, "I was absolutely certain I would never see it again."

Jack started to speak and Will waved one hand sharply to stop him.

"This was Mama's favorite house," Pa went on, his voice quiet and almost distant. "I believe because my father disliked it." At the word *father*, his jaw worked. "Mama kept us here, out of his sight, and we were happy."

"Why did you leave?" blurted Jack.

Pa stiffened in his saddle. "War," he said, his voice cold and flat. "One war after another." He glanced at Jack. "I was the second son, the spare, useless one. My father bought me a commission and told me not to humiliate him. The army put me on a ship to America, and..." He fell silent.

Jack was fidgeting. Again Will made an impatient motion to keep him quiet. He knew a little of what came next. A remote posting in the wilderness and a dangerous expedition into French territory that ended very badly, so badly his father changed his name and disappeared, allowing his family to believe him dead. He knew Jack *didn't* know any of that, but now might not be the best time to air the grievance again.

But Guy Montclair said nothing and finally the tension grew too great. "Pa?" Jack asked tentatively. "You told Will... Why not me?"

Their father blinked out of his reverie and looked between the two of them. "Oui," he said wryly. "I told you too little, and *you* too much." That last was at Will, who kept his mouth shut.

Pa glanced over his shoulder, then started his horse again, at a sedate walk. Without being told, Will and Jack guided their horses on either side of him. "I never meant to tell a soul, after it happened." Pa spoke haltingly. "Only your mother knows." He darted a sharp look at Will. "I know you want to tell your wife, but..." He paused. "If the duchess hears it, I must be the one to tell her." There seemed to be a shadow over his face. "I broke her heart."

"She's ready to forgive," said Will quietly. Philippa had been hammering away on this point for weeks, and she would know the duchess's true feelings.

"She doesn't yet know what she would have to forgive," returned Pa.

They rode several minutes in silence before Pa abruptly reined in his horse. "I will tell you once, and then I never wish to speak of it again." He was himself again, brisk and purposeful. "Oui? Swear to me. You will never say a word to my mother." He gave Will a hard look. "Swear to me you will *keep* this promise, in word and in deed, giving no hints or suggestive statements that betray it to her or to anyone who might tell her. Not one word."

Will flushed, but he and his brother both promised.

Pa took a deep breath. "I was sent into the army as a young man, as most second sons were. My father was tyrannical and a duke, so I was given no choice in the matter. I was glad to escape him, even at the cost of going into the army. My regiment was sent to America when the trouble began with the French, stirring up their allies among the native peoples against English colonists. We were stationed in Philadelphia for some months, then sent to reinforce a garrison in New York territory." He paused. "This was in 1757."

A premonition trickled through Will's mind.

"We were deep in the wilderness, miles from anything as civilized as Philadelphia or Boston, and the summer was unbearably hot. Black flies ate us alive, and the only respite was swimming in Lake George. The colonel was a fool, the captain worse. They disdained the American soldiers as unlearned farmers, far below the basest British soldier. But I... I had friends among them." A faint smile flickered across his mouth for a moment before vanishing. "I was nearly brought up before a court-martial for how friendly I was with the provincials, as the English called them. A man named Jack Deane was my closest friend, a Massachusetts man at home in the woods. He was what the Americans called a ranger, able to hunt and track as the native peoples did. General Webb recognized the value of the rangers' skills while wanting as little to do with them as possible. He instructed his men to learn from them, so that he would not have to rely on them." He sighed, his eyes distant. "I took to it with enthusiasm."

Yes, Will thought, *Pa would have.*

"I was assigned to accompany my captain and an orderly on a ranger scout. We sought intelligence of the French disposition. An attack was believed imminent, as the French General Montcalm was at Carillon, only forty miles away. The rangers dressed to conceal themselves, in brown and gray and green, but the captain insisted we were British officers and we would dress as such. He said he would have me flogged if I dared question his orders again." Even after more than thirty years, rage echoed in his voice.

"But we were successful. We discovered the French outposts without incident and counted their men and were making our way back south. It was so bloody hot. I disobeyed the captain and removed my red coat." He swallowed hard. "And then we came upon them. A pair of Frenchmen and an Iroquois guide. The rangers did not march through the forest in ranks, as the English did. They spread out and moved from tree to shrub to fallen log, and one of them had apprehended these fur traders, who were doing nothing more sinister than trying to endure the infernal heat. We could not afford to leave them free, as they might report to the French soldiers that we were about. We were still miles from Ford Edward.

"Deane brought them to us. They weren't soldiers or warriors, so Deane proposed leaving them bound, while we made haste to the fort. They would get free, but not before we were well away. The captain..." Pa's hands were shaking, and his horse tossed his head.

"The captain was furious. He was a cruel man, petty and jealous and vicious, who regarded the Indian natives as inhuman savages and the French as little better for allying with them, even though the British army also had native allies. He favored killing the captives, and he proved it by shooting one of the fur traders in the face." Pa's voice began to crack. "He was young, like me. He'd be sent into the army by his father, like me, and then became a trader to seek his fortune. He was beloved by his mother, like me, and a jolly companion to his friends—"

Abruptly Pa stopped his horse and leapt from the saddle. Will threw his own reins at his brother and bolted after him. He found his father bent over, vomiting into the ditch. He stopped, suddenly as frightened as a child might be by the sight of a parent's illness. His father had never appeared so vulnerable.

Jack rode up with the horses in tow, looking just as alarmed as Will. Pa took his horse's reins and wiped his mouth with a handkerchief Will offered.

"Captain Meachum shot that young Frenchman in the

face, coldly and callously. They were prisoners, not even soldiers, who had done nothing to us. It was inhumane, and Jack Deane went for Meachun with his knife. Meachum ran his sword through Deane's belly, and I... I put my hatchet into Meachum's back again and again until I knew for certain he was dead." Another spasm rippled across his face. "Deane was my friend. We were miles from any surgeon, little good though they were, and Meachum had stabbed him for no reason but that Deane questioned him."

Pa wiped his mouth again. From the corner of his eye, Will saw Jack draw breath to ask something. The quelling glare he turned on his brother was ferocious.

"The only witnesses were a French fur trader and an Iroquois, who had watched me hack Meachum to a bloody mess. The other rangers and the orderly would search for us, and I began to panic. I would be court-martialed and hanged. I had my knife in my hand, unsure if I would fight or simply cut my own throat, when the other Frenchman stopped me. He must have feared I was a madman, about to kill them, too, though I assured him I meant them no harm. But he was not a stupid man, and he had spent much time in military forts in the course of his travels. He knew what would happen to me."

Pa looked at them, his eyes hollow. "He said we could all escape if I took his friend's clothing and fled with them. Later he told me he feared the other English would lock him in a prison, or hang him on suspicion of being a French spy. And I... I was in the grip of a sort of madness. Even if my father had decided to bring his influence to bear and saved me from the rope, he would have punished me all the rest of his days for such dishonorable conduct. Captain Meachum was well-connected and had friends in Parliament who would want my blood. I thought I would prefer to be dead, and I became so."

"What was the young Frenchman's name?" asked Will softly. But he knew.

Pa took a deep breath. "Guillaume Montclair. I took his name and I took his life. I put on his clothing and put mine on him, including the red coat. Bazerac, the trader, told me I could take nothing, but I kept the medallion my mother had given me. Then Bazerac said a prayer over his friend, and bashed in his head until he was unrecognizable. We fled into the forest, and I thought it more likely than not that he or the Iroquois—whom Bazerac called Hawk—would eventually kill me, or at best leave me. Either would be fair justice for what I'd done. Instead they took me into Canada with them and taught me how to hunt, which skins were most profitable, and how to trade."

"But... why?" Jack wanted to know. "When the war was over..."

Pa smiled bitterly. "The war was not over for another six years. By then I had become Guy Montclair to my marrow. In my memories of that terrible day, his face had become my own, as if William St. James had truly died in that forest clearing. I had met your mother, on a trading journey to Montreal. We had you, our two small sons. I had fully accepted my new life, and the prospect of unearthing my old life filled me with terror. I did not know my father was dead, but his reach was long and his temper unforgiving." He looked at Will. "If anyone other than you had confronted me with the old name, I would have denied it and left England on the next ship, never to return."

"Did you ever wish to come back?" ventured Will.

Pa sighed. "As who? Guy Montclair, common Frenchman, would never have been welcomed here. But neither would Lord William St. James, who murdered a British officer. The longer I was away, the less I thought about it. I was certain Lord William had been long forgotten, better loved dead than he would be alive. The only thing I missed... Ah, I missed my brothers and my sister, and my mother. That, I did regret."

They gathered up their reins and began walking toward the castle. The sunlight had mellowed into the golden haze of a late summer afternoon. The castle was stunning at this time of day. Will took a deep breath, and realized he was glad to be home.

He wondered if his father felt the same.

"A Frenchman named Charles-Joseph LeVecque said he knew you," said Jack suddenly. "Could he have known the real—er, the original Guillaume Montclair?"

Pa frowned. "What was his age?"

"About yours, a little older. He said his friend had been a military man who'd gone to New France and been a fur trader. He was certain it was you, and that you would want us to accept his shipments..." Jack's voice died away.

Pa turned on him, brows raised. "You refused his shipments? Why?"

"He wanted us to ship guns and cannon to France, and recruit Americans to fight for him as his own private army in France," said Will. Jack kept his face averted.

Pa stopped in his tracks and slashed one hand. "Or course we will not ship guns and cannon! And to France! An enemy to the British, who harass American ships when they believe they can get away with it. Do I want my ships sunk or seized by a British frigate? No! You told him no, did you not?" he demanded. "Tell me you told him no."

"We did," said Will. Jack, cowed, mumbled something that sounded like agreement.

"Good." Pa's voice was firm and full again. He strode on, horse walking behind him. "Imbecile," he muttered. "We are not merchants of war. Do you have other questions? Ask, before the others catch us."

"Did you ever learn what happened, in your regiment, after your disappearance?"

For the first time Pa smiled. "A little, many years later. Deane did not die of his wound, even though he fell as senseless as if he were dead and had no memory of that day. He was discovered by the other rangers and taken back to the fort, where he somehow recovered enough to go home to Massachusetts. I saw him again, to our mutual shock. He had been unconscious, of course, when I exchanged my life for Guy Montclair's and fled, and he had believed me dead. I told him a few lies. I said I had wanted to escape the army and that was as suitable a chance as any. He accepted it, because he had been in the fort and he knew." He glanced at Jack. "You are named for him, Jacques."

"Not for the duke?" asked Will without thinking.

Eyes on the castle, Pa grinned a little. "Oui, also for my brother. Though he was never called Jack. He was Johnny, or—"

"Joffred," finished Will.

Pa laughed. "You remember that? No wonder someone found you out. It must have been a mighty struggle to keep your mouth closed, eh?" He smirked knowingly at Will's frown. "Especially when a lovely lady decided to pry out your secrets."

"I can keep a secret," growled Will.

Jack hooted. "Not very well! I knew you were hopeless

the moment I saw her! You couldn't keep a secret from Philippa to save your life—"

Will rounded on him. "Quiet!"

Pa laughed again. "No, no, I am very glad to hear it." His smile lingered as he looked at Will. "I can forgive the lies and secrets because you have given me back something I thought I had lost forever." Then he added, more sternly, "But do not ever do it again."

P hilippa and the duchess had discussed at great length how to break the incredible news of Lord William's return to the duke. The duchess hadn't wanted to tell him before they went to London, in case Lord William hadn't agreed to come to Carlyle, but the duke remembered what they'd told him about Will's identity, and he kept asking about Will's father. The duchess worried the shock would harm him. Philippa argued that Carlyle would be so pleased, he would recover.

In the end, Will suggested the best way. "He thought I was my father when I simply wandered into the garden. He was surprised but not alarmed or shocked, and he called me over to sit with him. Now His Grace almost expects to see Pa."

The duchess had looked at Philippa, who nodded. "That sounds as reasonable as anything else."

Lord William had agreed. Philippa still hadn't figured him out. He was charming to her and gentle with the duchess, but she had the feeling he was like Will, capable of dissembling charm even while concealing immense inner strain. Both he and his wife—who called him Guy, to the duchess's discomfort—had been polite, charming, and guarded, but Will swore up and down that his father was looking forward to seeing the duke again.

Now Philippa strained to see from the window onto the duke's private terrace in the Tulip Garden. The duchess had her face almost pressed to the glass. Carlyle had recovered from his illness, and Philippa was privately certain that learning Will's true identity had helped in that. Now Will and the duke were sitting in the sun with Mr. Amis, eating cakes and drinking tea. An empty chair sat beside the duke's chaise.

Mrs. Montclair came up beside Philippa. "He is going now," she said softly.

"Is he worried?"

Her mother-in-law smiled. "No. He and Jack went for a long ride, to settle his nerves."

Philippa nodded and went back to the window. To her mild surprise, Léonie Montclair turned away and sat down. "Do—do you not wish to see?" she whispered.

"I know how it will go," said the other woman with a wry look. She picked up the copy of *Gulliver's Travels* and paged through it.

The duchess inhaled, and Philippa whirled back to the window. Guy Montclair came striding around the corner of the castle, whistling, as if he did it every day. At his approach, Will raised one hand. Philippa pushed the casement open just an inch; they didn't want to be caught spying, but the duchess was so anxious about this...

"Ah! Lemuel!" cried the duke in delighted astonishment. "I've been expecting you."

"I stayed away until you would forget our last wager," said Guy easily. "You have, haven't you, Joffred?"

After a stunned moment, the duke gave a faint laugh. "I

suppose I have. Which is unfortunate, as I'm sure I won it. Come, sit and remind me what we wagered..."

Philippa let out her breath. The duchess's eyes were closed, and her lips trembled. After a moment she gave a nod and came away from the window with Philippa.

"Shall I ring for tea?" Philippa asked brightly. The world had grown five degrees warmer and vastly happier in the space of two minutes.

"Please, Pippa." The duchess turned to Mrs. Montclair. "How did you know how it would go?"

Mrs. Montclair smiled. "I know my husband. I know my son. They are both very good at sensing what others are thinking or feeling, and responding appropriately."

At that the duchess's eyes flashed. "Indeed."

"Yes, I believe my son perceived exactly your regard for him, and he deliberately provoked you to dislike him," said the woman with an apologetic expression. "He did not want you to know him. My husband... he wants his brother to know him."

From outdoors came the sound of laughter.

The duchess relented. "I only want him to be pleased. The duke... does not remember well."

Mrs. Montclair nodded in understanding. "I believe that will be a comfort to my husband. He remembers far *too* well sometimes."

That night Philippa asked Will about it. She had moved into Stone Cottage upon their marriage, even though the duchess was fretting that another, finer, house must be built for them. Philippa liked Stone Cottage, and it was convenient for Will, who was still acting as estate steward. There was only room at Stone Cottage for her and Will and Marianne, but they were near enough to visit the castle every day. It was their private world.

Will grinned at her question. "Oh yes, Pa's a great charmer. He take a genuine interest in other people, and easily picks up enthusiasms. Talk to him of your favorite subject, and he will ask question after question until you're utterly persuaded he's as fascinated by it as you are."

Philippa laughed. "The duchess is very pleased."

Will pulled his shirt over his head and tossed it aside. They were dressing for bed. "All the better for me, if Pa can please her."

She scoffed as he bent and put his mouth on the side of her neck. "You could please her yourself, if you would try..."

"I think I've done her a good turn or two," he murmured against her skin. Philippa let her head fall to the side as his hands crept into her unbound hair.

"You have," she whispered. "Unspeakably good turns."

Then she put her arms around him and took him to bed.

"You must stay on the path," Will instructed. "Going out of bounds will disqualify you."

Philippa nodded, flexing her hands. "Right."

"You can kick the ground with your feet. You may not kick the other person or the other horse."

"As if I would!" protested Sophie.

"I know you," he said sternly.

She squawked in outrage. "William Montclair! How dare you!"

"Get on with it," called the Duke of Carlyle from his seat in the landau, some twenty feet away. "We were promised a race!"

"Hear, hear!" Guy Montclair clapped loudly.

"Setting the rules, sir," Will called back. He turned to them again and lowered his voice. "Don't crash. That's what matters most. One or both of them will fly at us in a fury if we destroy these horses."

Philippa laughed. She sat astride Nestor, his worn leather saddle replaced with a polished new one and his scraggly mane replenished. Beside her, Sophie sat on Hengroen, who had been located in the attics and given his own refurbishment.

There had been a great deal of argument and excitement over this race. Once Guy learned that Will's knowledge of the wooden horses had helped prove his identity to the duchess, he'd led a search of the castle for the missing Hengroen. Then he and Carlyle had told story after story of their childhood, including some that made the duchess exclaim in shock and indignation while Philippa and Sophie laughed so hard they cried.

Will and Jack had wanted to race the horses, of course, and Carlyle and Guy heartily approved. The duchess had vetoed that at once. "You are much too old, and far too heavy," she'd told them severely. "Those horses are meant for *children*, and I will not have the two of you destroy them before my great-grandchildren have a chance to ride them."

Jack retreated at once—he was still cowed by the duchess—but Philippa knew how to handle her. It took her less than half an hour to persuade the duchess that Sophie, at seventeen, was still a child who deserved a chance to ride the horses, and the two of them were far smaller and lighter than either Will or Jack, and how much pleasure would it give the duke and his brother to see their steeds in action once again?

So here they were. The duchess and the duke watched from the landau. Mr. Montclair paced beside the carriage, muttering to the duke; Philippa was sure they were making wagers on the outcome. Mrs. Montclair had helped Sophie tuck up her skirts and was whispering instructions in her ear. Will came over and put his arm around her before leaning down to do the same.

"Sophie will try to cut you off," he breathed. "Do not let her."

"She would not!"

"That's what my mother is telling her to do." He kissed her cheek, his lips lingering by her ear. "If you lose, we will obviously need to race again."

"Lose!" She gasped in outrage. "You think I will lose?"

He shrugged. "I know my family. A more competitive lot you've never met."

Philippa glanced at Sophie. The girl's face was bright with eagerness, but when she smiled back at Philippa, her eyes glinted with mischievous cunning.

She turned back to her husband. "You forget one thing," she whispered to him, so softly he had to lean down and put his ear right in front of her lips. "I know every inch of this estate, including this path, and she does not." She nipped his earlobe lightly between her teeth. "And when I want something, I get it."

He shuddered. When he looked at her, his eyes glinted gold with desire. "Perhaps we should also make a wager on this race..."

She laughed, leaned forward, and whispered her wager in his ear. Will swallowed, lurched upright and waved his arms. "Time to race! Come, Mama, we haven't got all day to strategize, let them run!"

Philippa tightened her grip on Nestor. There were reins, but for this she and Sophie held the wooden pegs at the sides of the horses' heads. Her skirts were pulled up securely through her pockets, and she focused intently on the wide curving path that led down the hill around the western wall of the castle.

Will dropped his arm and they were off with whoops and cries from the spectators. Dimly Philippa heard Will shouting, but she was digging in her toes to generate speed before the slope of the hill cut sharply downward and then she was flying, bent low over Nestor's neck, her knees clamped tight to his wooden sides, her feet tucked up behind her away from the rattling wheels and spray of dirt and gravel from the road.

She *did* know this path. She'd walked it, ridden it, run it, rolled her hoop up and down it a thousand times. She remembered the rut that ran from left to right, following the flow of water away from the castle gutter. She remembered the subtle bump from the roots of the towering oak tree, even though the tree stood thirty feet from the path. She remembered that the path was slightly banked to make it easier on carriages going down the hill, and she leaned into the turn to guide Nestor around it.

Behind her she heard a shriek of frustration. Sophie had caught the rut and fallen behind. Philippa kicked twice more and sailed down, past the oak tree, onto the raked gravel drive at the front of the castle. She was sitting on Nestor, breathless and laughing, when Will dashed up beside her on Gringolet.

"Masterful race!" He leapt down and lifted her off the horse, spinning them both around. "Brilliant!"

Philippa wound her arms around his neck, grinning. "I told you I knew what to do."

Sophie had run aground on the grass nearby. The landau pulled up behind her, and Guy Montclair vaulted over the side even before it stopped, earning a rebuke from the duchess. He ran to crouch over Hengroen with Sophie, followed by his wife.

"They are plotting how to fix Hengroen for a better run," Will murmured.

Philippa shook her head. "Nestor is too old for this! Let him end his racing career as a champion. We must design and build our own new horse, if there are to be more races."

His eyes brightened. "A *larger* horse."

She laughed. "Large enough to hold you?"

"Obviously."

Behind them, the duke was crowing in victory and calling them to come celebrate Nestor's triumph. Even the duchess was smiling. Will rested his forehead against hers, suddenly somber. "Thank you, my love."

"For helping the duke win yet another wager over your father?"

He made an amused grimace. "Yes... and for everything else. Seeing through me. Loving me anyway. Persuading me this might all work."

She wove her fingers into his hair. "There was no other way for us to have each other. All this"—she waved one arm behind her, at the castle, at their companions, at Carlyle—"had to fall in line, so I made it. I told you, I know how to get what I want."

He laughed again. "Thank God for that."

. . .

L éonie Montclair hung back as everyone else made their way down the stairs.

They had been here for several days now, and she still had no sense of direction in the castle. The duchess had assigned a personal maid to her and Sophie, merely to help them dress, which was almost as jarring as sleeping in a room built for jousting knights.

She was not at all certain she liked this place.

"We will be late for dinner," said her husband behind her.

"Guy," she said fondly, touching his face.

He stopped on the stairs at her side. "What is wrong?"

She laughed, embarrassed. Everyone would think her mad if she complained about having a personal maid and living in a castle with an aristocratic husband. "Nothing." She paused, looking around. "Are you happy to be here?"

She hadn't asked him yet. Ever since Will had met them in that London inn near the docks, his face grave and anxious, and began to explain what he'd done, Léonie had held her tongue.

Partly, as a mother. She could see the hope in her son's eyes, and she realized how much he wanted forgiveness and acceptance, even though he'd broken his word to Guy. Will spoke of the lady he had married, and Léonie recognized that her child was in love—and that he was staying here, no matter what the rest of them said or did.

So she held her tongue and listened as her husband shouted at Will, with Will answering quietly, Jack attempting to pipe up from time to time and getting shouted at in turn. She knew Guy's secret; she had known it since the day before she married him, when he confessed that he had once been not a French fur trader but an English gentleman who murdered a man, and she had married him anyway. She knew his lost family had been a stone of regret in his heart, even as their life in America flourished with success and love. And she knew that if he wanted to come home, to see his mother and brother again, she would go with him and support him.

But she sincerely hoped he did not want to return and live in this luxurious dungeon.

He took her hand and pressed it to his cheek for a moment. They slowly started down the stairs, hand in hand. She had always known him as Guillaume, always called him Guy, and now everyone was calling him Lord William. One maid tried to call *her* Lady William, and Léonie had put a quick end to that. She did not like these exalted titles.

"I am very happy to see my family again," he said. "If only Jessica and Stephen—" He stopped, and she squeezed his hand.

"It cannot be changed." She looked around again. "But everything else... It could be. Do you wish to remain here?"

He rocked back on his heels. "If I did, would you stay, too?"

She shrugged. He was teasing her, and she was repaying him. "Perhaps. Perhaps not."

He grinned. "There's a tower. I could lock you in it..."

She raised one brow. "Much good would that do you, if I decided to leave."

"I know it." He slid his arm around her waist, pulling her close. "I would work very hard to dissuade you from leaving me, though."

She smiled at that. "I know." They had reached the ground floor of the soaring central hall. The marble floor, the carved woodwork, the vaulted stone ceiling were all very impressive. "Will intends to stay."

"Oh yes, we've lost him to Carlyle." He hesitated, then spoke slowly. "He wants me to resume my place as Johnny's heir. So that this will all be his, some day."

"Do you want to do that?"

Guy scratched his chin. "I see little reason not to. Between the two of them, he and Philippa are already managing everything. Nothing would be required of me except a signature here and there." He looked at her. "And he wants it so badly. He wants out of the shipping business, and Jack would be very pleased to see him go as well. Jack likes living in London. He will do well there, given some time and experience. I can satisfy both of them at once by agreeing to this. Besides, it can hardly hurt our business to have a ducal connection."

She let out her breath in relief; her shoulders eased. "So you would only do it for Will?"

"Why else?" he asked in surprise. "I don't want this. My home is in Boston, with you. My *life* is with you."

Léonie was surprised how strongly her heart leapt at that statement. "So we will only stay to visit," she said, smiling broadly. "And then go home."

He gave her the deceptively mild look, the one she knew meant trouble. "Oui, ma chérie. I always meant to take you home. Who would want to live here?"

As one they turned to regard the marble statue in the curve of the stairs behind them. It was of Perseus, striding forward in victory, the monstrous head of Medusa dangling from his outstretched hand.

"It is hideous," said Léonie quietly but fervently.

"Unspeakably," agreed her husband. "It terrified me as a

child. I'll tell Will I'll do as he wants, if he swears an oath to take a hammer and chisel to that monstrosity."

She looked at him, and he looked at her, his eyebrow up in that wicked way, and she choked on a laugh. "I don't believe you would make a very good duke," she whispered.

"Absolutely wretched," he agreed with relish. "Let's go to dinner, my love. My mother always did keep a fine table, and we should enjoy it while we are here."

CHAPTER 5

THE DUCHESS

Sophia Constance St. James, Duchess of Carlyle, sat in her chair and surveyed the room. Percival lay in her lap, purring softly.

On a cushion at her feet, paging through one of Jessica's old books about India, sat her granddaughter Sophie. Her heart swelled; her granddaughter *Sophia*, who had her own dark eyes and sharp mind. Her grandsons were listening to her sons telling tall tales—she was sure many of them could not possibly be true—and Philippa was blatantly encouraging their boasting. William's wife Léonie was listening with a faint, knowing smile, as if she knew even wilder tales.

Her Grace hoped she was permitted to hear some of them, some day. William had not told her what happened in America, why he had let them all think him dead for thirty years. She could see it had been a weight on his shoulders for so long, it had sunk into his very bones, and was not something he could disburden easily.

She would wait. That day in London, only three weeks

ago, waiting for him to walk through the door, hardly daring to believe he ever could, the duchess had felt every bit of the pain that had torn her heart when the letter arrived decades ago, saying he was dead in America. The general had written that her son—her William, with his ready laugh and high spirits and unquenchable thirst for adventure—had been mauled by French savages, so severely he could only be identified by his regimental coat. Pacing Diana Beauchamp's parlor, waiting, praying, *hoping*, had been so agonizing she'd feared she would have an apoplexy and drop on the spot.

None of that mattered now. He was alive. He was *home*. She had made a promise to God that if He returned William to her, she would never, ever ask what had kept him away. But she still hoped he would tell her, some day.

Tonight the castle, which had seemed on the brink of melancholy and grief, was instead filled with laughter and family. Johnny hadn't been in such good health and spirits for years. He rode out in the carriage almost every day now, and dined with them regularly. He had accepted his brother's reappearance contentedly, as if the thirty year absence had been nothing more than a bad prank, and was delighted to have two nephews and a niece.

And she... She had *grandchildren*. As sorry as she was not to have known them earlier, her heart was full to bursting with love for them now. Sophie was mischievous, like her father had been; Jack was more like Johnny, honest and good but willing to be caught up in trouble if someone else led the way. Will... She had to press her lips together at the thought of how he'd provoked her.

But if he hadn't come, if he hadn't annoyed her and vexed her so he could remain undiscovered at the castle, if he hadn't teased and flirted with Philippa... None of this would have happened. She was still vexed with the young man, but deep down she was coming to love him anyway.

The duchess's gaze caught on the portrait on the wall, the one that had shown Philippa the truth. How well she remembered the month it took to paint that. Johnny had just finished at Oxford, excelling in history, while William had been on the verge of being sent down for misbehavior. Jessica had been ten, perpetually escaping her governess to climb trees or hide away with a book, and her dear sweet Stephen had been three, cranky from his teeth coming in. It had been a long, hot month, when all their tempers frayed as the painter, Mr. Hudson, and his assistant fussed and scolded.

But it had also been a happy month, one of the last times they were all together. Johnny and William had played pranks on each other and spoiled Jessica outlandishly, pushing her on the wooden swing in the garden and taking her for long punts on the river. Jessica had staged nightly speeches arguing that she ought to be allowed to go away to school like her brothers, and Stephen had made them all laugh by chasing after the cat who was Percival's six-times-great-grandmother.

Johnny had gone off to the Continent a few weeks later, not to return for almost three years. By the time he was home, William had scraped through Oxford and been sent into the army with a lieutenant's commission. When he came home next on leave, Stephen had just departed for Eton, and Jessica, who had won her way in the end, was halfway through her two years at a young ladies' academy before her debut. Johnny had been traveling from estate to estate at his father's command, dutifully learning the management he would never use. Then William had been lost, followed a year later by his father, and then Johnny's accident.

She sighed. So much she wished she'd known. So many years she'd regretted... too much.

But now God had smiled on her and given her back an infinitely precious piece of what she'd lost.

She raised her eyes to the portrait again. There hadn't been one painted of the family since. But now, she decided, she needed a new one—no, *several* new portraits. One of William and his family. One of Johnny, at long last, even though she feared he and William would conspire to have him painted in the guise of Robinson Crusoe or some ridiculous thing. One of Will and Philippa, just married; they made such a very handsome couple.

Her Grace's fond gaze lingered a moment on Philippa. She thanked God that Colonel Kirkpatrick had brought his small daughter home to England before he fell in love with Jessica. Without Philippa, the duchess was certain her heart would have given out from the sorrows she'd endured. Philippa had brought joy and comfort and purpose to her life when everything else had been dark and melancholy. She was not Jessica's daughter in blood, but most certainly in spirit. Jessica would have been immensely proud of Philippa —as was the duchess herself.

Yes, she would want another portrait to hang opposite the Hudson portrait, of all of them—she with her two sons, her daughter-in-law, her granddaughter and two grandsons, and her beloved Philippa.

The cat in her lap stretched, and the duchess smiled as

she scratched his neck. Even Percival would be in this portrait.

She would direct Mr. Edwards to begin searching for an artist as soon as he returned from his holiday.

ABOUT A KISS

CHAPTER 1

The best thing that ever happened to Christopher Lawrence was getting sacked.

He hadn't thought so at the time, when his employer, Lord Percy Willoughby was frantically throwing belongings into a trunk and shouting at him to hire a carriage. His main hope, of being paid his wages owed, was dashed when Lord Percy rushed out the door, mumbling a half-hearted promise that he would send for Lawrence as soon as he smoothed things over with his father.

Kit knew that for a lie. Lord Percy would be quite some time explaining this mess to the Earl of Hulme. He had returned from Vauxhall Gardens the previous morning, so drunk he was barely on his own two feet, moaning about a disastrous run of cards. The scribbled debts of honor had been presented the following morning and sent Lord Percy haring back to Northumberland.

Which left Kit unemployed and desperate when Maximilian St. James offered him a position. He'd accepted on the spot.

Aside from recognizing Mr. St. James as a friend of Lord Percy's, Kit knew little about him. Another gambler, he'd supposed, probably a rogue, too. He'd resigned himself to seeking another position within the year.

It turned out, though, that Mr. St. James needed a valet because he was to be married. Kit was somewhat confused about who the bride was, but when all was said and done, he found himself installed in a quaint half-timbered cottage in the tiny town of Marslip, sharing the laundry and the servants' stair with a girl called Jennie Hickson, lady's maid to the new Mrs. St. James.

After that, Mr. St. James could have stopped paying him, cursed him and thrown things at him, and Kit would have stayed. Because Jennie was there.

***

CHAPTER 2

Jennie Hickson was elated to be promoted to lady's maid. At Perusia Hall, where her parents were butler and housekeeper and her cousin Ellen was ladies' maid to the Misses Tate, she had only been Ellen's assistant. That meant she was assigned the worst chores, like laundry and mending, while Ellen got to learn hair arranging and how to make cosmetics.

When Miss Cathy Tate was supposed to marry Mr. St. James, Ellen had begun instructing Jennie in those skills, somewhat smugly. Ellen was a bit full of herself, soon to be maid to Mrs. St. James, while Jennie would be left behind at Perusia Hall.

Then Miss Tate eloped in the night with the curate, Miss Bianca married Mr. St. James in her sister's place, and everything was turned on its head. Now Jennie was moving to Poplar House with the new and unexpected Mrs. St. James, while Ellen was left to sulk at Perusia Hall with no lady to attend at all, which reduced her to parlor maid.

"Are you ready for this, daughter?" her mother asked as Jennie excitedly bundled up her possessions.

"As ready as ever, Mam! 'Tis still Miss Bianca, whom I've waited on these ten years."

Her mother raised an eyebrow. "Waited on, when she never wanted her hair done or an elegant dress! You've had it easy, Jennie, and now she's a married lady. It won't be the same."

"Mam!" Jennie laughed. "Didn't you hear her going at it with Mr. Tate this morning? She's the same as she was."

Mrs. Hickson frowned in reproof. "Aye, but Mr. St. James is a London gentleman. He'll want his wife dressed finer than any Marslip lady. And mark my words, no matter how they cut up at each other today"—no one had missed the black looks Miss Bianca had given her new husband at the wedding breakfast—"she'll come around. Miss Bianca—no, Mrs. St. James!—has a good heart. She won't stay angry at him forever."

Jennie rolled her eyes. "I know! And here I am, your own daughter, hoping to hear you wish me luck, instead of hearing all the ways I'm not ready and not good enough."

At this her mother smiled. "Of course you are! You're ready, and good, and I am very proud of you." She hugged Jennie and kissed her cheek. "Say farewell to your papa and be on your way. Mustn't keep Mrs. St. James waiting!"

Jennie laughed, and her father helped carry her things down the hill to Poplar House and into her little room at the top of the back stairs. The window looked out on the hill toward Perusia Hall. She gazed at it and smiled as her father pointed out that she could see her parents' windows in the servants' wing from here. "Give us a wave now and then,

Jennie," he said as he hugged her before heading back to the main house.

She hummed as she unpacked her things. Ellen had bragged about this room, thinking it would be hers. It was neat and comfortable, and larger than her old room in Perusia. Jennie grinned at herself in the small mirror, adjusting her cap. She could hear Mrs. St. James's voice floating up the stairwell from the kitchen, meaning she had best hurry down.

She stepped out onto the narrow landing and came face-to-face with a man coming up the stairs. "Oh! Sorry!" she said instinctively.

He stopped cold. "For what?"

Jennie blinked. Down a step, he was the same height as she was. He was young, probably about Miss Bianca's age, with copper skin and close-cut black hair, and sinfully long eyelashes. "I beg your pardon, miss, but you did me no wrong." He stepped aside to let her by.

Jennie blushed. "You must be Mr. St. James's man."

He managed a graceful bow, even in the cramped stairwell. "Christopher Lawrence, miss."

"Oh!" She laughed from nerves, him bowing to her like she was a lady. "Jennie Hickson, sir. I do for Mrs. St. James."

He smiled again, his teeth white and perfect. "A pleasure to make your acquaintance, Miss Hickson. Please call me Kit."

She blushed harder, till she could feel the heat in her face. "Oh, right! Great pleasure. Kit? Kit. Call me Jennie," she squeaked, and slipped past him.

Down the stairs she clattered, fanning herself with one hand. Goodness, Mam hadn't warned her about *this*. Mr. St. James's man was fearfully handsome.

CHAPTER 3

For the first few weeks in Marslip, Kit kept his guard up, trying to learn his new employer's ways.

St. James and his wife did not get on well. That was plain to see from the frosty looks the lady gave him, and the barbed words they exchanged.

It was just as plain that Mr. St. James found his wife much more appealing than she found him. His gaze would follow her across the room, and he would stop speaking for a moment if her voice floated through the wall that divided their bedrooms.

Kit found that promising. All the money in the marriage, he had quickly learned, came from the bride's family. If the pair of them separated, Kit could easily find himself on the streets again. But as long as Mr. St. James stole those hungry, intense looks at his wife when he thought no one was watching, there was a good chance the man would sort out how to win her affections.

Kit quickly fell into an easy camaraderie with the other servants. Mary, the downstairs maid, was friendly and helpful. Cook was a kindly woman whose tarts and puddings made his eyes roll back in his head in ecstasy. And Jennie...

Jennie made his heart leap.

She had curly black hair and big brown eyes and a habit of humming as she worked. She laughed a great deal and was treated by her mistress more like a younger sister than a maid. When not attending Mrs. St. James, Jennie spent her time in the kitchen, mending and shelling peas and chattering with Mary and Cook.

And amazingly enough, Jennie seemed as intrigued by him as he was by her. When he sat down to repair the lace on Mr. St. James's ivory satin coat, torn after the wedding, Jennie leaned over to watch how he did it. Kit showed her.

"Pick up the threads on the point, see?" He demonstrated, weaving the needle through the ragged lace threads. "Then pull, but lightly or it won't lie smooth."

She sat back, looking impressed. "You do fine work."

He laughed, finishing the repair. "Adequate! Anyone who looks closely will spot it." He bit off the thread and winked at her. "But they *will* have to look closely."

"Miss Bianca—that is, Mrs. St. James—never went in for much lace, and when she does wear it, she takes care. Nary a spot or a tear." Jennie was fixing a cloak hem, ripped out from being stepped on.

"I don't envy those ladies' maids in London," Kit replied. "So much lace and embroidery, and the kerchiefs made of gauze! My mother said they're as delicate as spiderwebs, and just as simple to mend."

"Is she in service, then? Your mum?"

"She was." Kit threaded his needle anew and set about reattaching a button. "Now she tends my sister's children, which I suppose is more than service."

"Oh?" Jennie wiggled forward eagerly in her seat, and Kit felt an unwarranted bolt of pleasure. "What about your pa?"

"Purser on a trading ship."

She drew back admiringly. "A world explorer! And I've never been out of Staffordshire."

Kit grinned. "Where would you go?"

"Spain," she said at once. "Or Italy. Or Turkey, to see the palaces, or America, to see the wilderness. Even Scotland!" She sighed. "Seeing Liverpool is probably the best I'll ever do —if I even get *that* far."

"What about London?" Mr. St. James had already told him they were going to town soon on business.

Jennie's eyes grew luminous. "Wouldn't that be lovely! What's it like? You lived there, aye?"

"Aye." He smiled back at her. Jennie's wide-eyed enthusiasm for everything had thoroughly charmed him. "You'll like it."

She blinked. "But—no, I won't be going. Mrs. St. James is attached to Perusia and her workshop. I'll be right here, mending and ironing..."

Kit leaned closer. "I bet you sixpence he'll find a way to persuade her to come, and then you'll have to come, too," he whispered.

"I shouldn't wager." She sat back, but her eyes still shone. "Sixpence?"

He waited hopefully.

She laughed. "Oh, you're a wicked one, Mr. Lawrence, but I'll take that bet. And hope I lose!"

"So will I," he replied. If he had to spend a month in London, let Jennie be there, too.

CHAPTER 4

As it happened, she did lose. With eyes like saucers she came down a few days later and told him. "I owe you sixpence."

Kit stopped blacking the boot in his hand and grinned. "Knew you would."

She flapped one hand at him with a fleeting smile. "Did you really know?"

He shrugged. "I guessed."

She sat down next to him, her skirt flowing over his shoes. Kit tried not to twitch. "What will it be like?"

He leaned forward, and she responded in kind. She smelled softly of lavender water, which she sprinkled on the clothes before ironing them. He loved the way she smelled on ironing days. "Busy."

Her pretty pink lips parted, and then she burst out laughing. "Of course it will be! But how? What is town like? Are there thieves on every corner and children starving in every alley? Do the King and Queen come out where folks can see them? Tell me!"

Kit grinned. "I doubt we'll see the King or the Queen, but I daresay you'll see many fine shops, the park, Pall Mall, the market...and whatever you do on your days out."

"Oh my," she gasped. "I didn't think of that! What did you do on your days out?"

Kit shrugged. He'd gone to boxing matches, both to watch and to fight. Lord Percy hadn't minded and had even gone along and watched him fight a few times. Wagered on him, too, which Kit had not liked. The last thing he'd needed was to be blamed for one of Lord Percy's gambling losses. "I could show you the Museum, in Great Russell Street," he offered. "And St. Paul's."

"Would you?" she asked, in such a tone of wonderment that Kit's blithe agreement faded on his tongue. He looked at her, and saw realization dawning in her eyes.

She realized he fancied her.

He waited, tense, afraid to speak and spoil his chance.

Slowly, hesitantly, she smiled. "Would you?" she repeated, softer and with an undercurrent of hope.

"I would." His mouth curved in spite of himself. "I would very much like to."

"Well." She looked down, her cheeks pink. "I shall ask Mrs. St. James if we might have the same day out."

He was very proud of himself for staying in his seat, one arm still inside the half-polished boot, and not leaping up with a euphoric shout. "'Tis a plan, then."

CHAPTER 5

Jennie seized the first excuse she could find to bolt up the hill to Perusia Hall. Her father said her mother was in the linen closet, and Jennie ran up the stairs.

Mrs. Hickson popped out of the closet, a frown on her face. "Jennie! Why be you clattering about like a boy?"

"Mam, oh Mam, we're going to London!" she burst out, too excited to apologize.

"What?" came a cry of dismay from the closet. Ellen appeared in the doorway, a half-folded sheet in her hands. "London?"

Oh dear, she hadn't realized Ellen was there. She forced herself to calm down. "Yes. Mr. St. James has business in town, and Mrs. St. James decided to go, too."

Ellen's eyes filled with tears. Mrs. Hickson patted her shoulder and handed her a stack of linen from the shelf near the door. "Take these down to the laundry, Ellen. They need boiling."

Slump-shouldered, her feet dragging, Ellen took the pile of yellowed linens and went down the back stairs. Mrs.

Hickson waited until she was out of sight, then pulled Jennie into the closet and shut the door.

"London!" she said, half excited, half worried. "And you're to go, too?"

Jennie nodded eagerly. "For a month."

Her mother bit her lip, but then smiled and folded her into an embrace. "You must be doing just fine, if Miss Bianca wants you with her in London."

"Have you been there, Mam?" she demanded.

"No, never. Your father's been, twice, but not for many years. You should ask him about it."

"I will." She hesitated. "Ellen's fair disappointed, isn't she?"

Her mother sighed. "Ellen's had her share of disappointment lately. She'll be right again when Miss Cathy comes home. When do you leave?"

"Within the week. Mam, Kit—that is, Mr. Lawrence says he'll show me St. Paul's on our day out. Isn't that kind of him?"

"Hmm, very kind of *Kit*," said her mother with a thoughtful glance.

Jennie blushed, but it was dim in the closet and she hoped her mother wouldn't see. "He's left already, to make arrangements. He used to live in London, of course, before he came to Mr. St. James..."

"And he's a kind one, is he?"

"Yes."

"And a handsome one," added her mother.

"Mam!" Now there was no way her blush would be unnoticed.

"What? You think I lost my eyesight when I married your papa?" Mam raised her brows. "And who are his people?"

"His mother was lady's maid to a planter's wife on Antigua," said Jennie. "And she worked for several ladies in London and Liverpool when she came to Britain. She taught him how to mend and clean something amazing, Mam! You'd be dazzled by how he fixes lace. And his pa is a ship's purser, sailing around the world."

"Hmph." But Mrs. Hickson's eyes were soft. "And it's his skill with lacework you admire, is it?"

Jennie straightened. "Of course." Then she couldn't stop a small grin. "As you said, he's also marvelously handsome!"

Her mother laughed and embraced her. "You be watchful of him, when you're off in London. Those London macaronis will break your heart."

"Mam. He's not a macaroni."

"All the same," said her mother, "you be watchful."

Jennie was. When they reached London several days later and Kit was waiting in the hall of a tall, elegant house, she watched him. She watched him as he ran errands for Mr. St. James, and handled the London servants, and managed the busy schedule Mr. St. James kept. He was unfailingly calm, capable, and good-humored. It was hard *not* to watch him, and she liked him more and more.

On their first half day out, he kept his promise and took her to the museum at Montagu House. Mindful of her mother's warning, Jennie wondered if he would try anything, but aside from offering his arm at times, he treated her as if she were a great lady. They wandered the museum together, marveling and sometimes gawking at the curiosities displayed there, especially the collection of objects from the South Seas.

"Could you imagine what it would be like, to see such people?" she asked softly as they regarded a remarkable costume bearing a label of "Mourning Costume, from Tahiti."

"I used to think I would do like Captain Cook, and sail around the world to see it all," he replied. "I wanted to see Antigua, where my mother was raised, and India. My father says India is one of the most beautiful places on earth, with beasts we never see here in Britain."

"But you didn't."

"No." He gave her a funny little smile. "Thankfully."

For some reason that made Jennie's heart skip a beat. "And now you can only see it in a museum with me."

He shrugged, but a flush crept up his tawny cheek. "I rather like it that way."

CHAPTER 6

Kit loved London.

Not for the dirt, or the noise, but for the energy of the city and the steady stream of things happening and because Jennie was constantly coming to him to ask advice.

"Mrs. St. James needs new stockings, where shall I buy some?" she would ask one day. "Mrs. St. James wants her hair powdered for the dinner tonight, where do I get powder?" was another question. Then the next night, "How can I get out this pomade from her gown?"

And Kit would direct her to the right shop or show her how to lift grease from silk. She was even fun to work with, humming some tune slightly off-key as she sponged and dabbed at stains, making him laugh with her occasional exclamations of frustration or delight.

When the St. Jameses decided to go to Vauxhall with some of Mr. St. James's friends, Kit felt a tremor of alarm. Not only was that where Lord Percy had met his downfall, it was clear Mr. St. James had once been very like Lord Percy: notorious at Vauxhall.

Muting his alarm was the fact that Mr. St. James had been sober and steady in all the time Kit had worked for him, and that the man really did not want to go to Vauxhall. It was Mrs. St. James who was keen to see the pleasure garden at night.

"She's trying to ruin me," he said morosely to Kit, of the Countess Dalway, who had invited them.

Kit sympathized. He also associated Vauxhall with ruin. But since Mrs. St. James wanted to go, they would go. Kit suspected his master was unable to deny his wife.

Jennie was almost as excited about the outing. "Oh, Kit, she spoke of wearing fancy dress, and how the fine ladies go dressed as queens and goddesses!" she told him. "Can you imagine?"

He could. "Do you know what Madam will wear?"

Jennie had shaken her head, but her impish smile suggested she had an idea. "It'll be splendid, though!"

As it happened, she was. When Mrs. St. James swept down the stairs in a black satin gown looking like Queen Elizabeth, Kit noted how stunned the lady's husband looked. *That'll keep him out of trouble,* he thought, and went to find Jennie, who was in raptures over the gown and the paste jewels and the *hair*.

"Mrs. Farquhar's maid, Thérèse, showed me how to dress it—even Ellen doesn't know the like!" She heaved a huge sigh of contentment. "I feel like a real Londoner now!"

Kit laughed. "Good. Come with me, you fine London miss."

She took his hand and let him lead her up up up the stairs. With their employers away for the night, they had the evening free. Kit led her through the narrow hallway past the servants' rooms on the top floor, and pushed open a window at the back of the house. The roof leveled off outside, and he scrambled out, helping Jennie behind him.

"Oh my!" She clutched his arm and stared, open-mouthed at the view.

London spread in front of them, lamps winking in the indigo blue twilight. The dome of St. Paul's glowed in the distance, presiding over a city settling down to sleep or to revels, depending on the citizen. Up here the air was cool and fresh.

Kit produced a bottle and two glasses from beside the chimney. "Since you're a real Londoner now, you should have some champagne."

Jennie's eyes grew wide. "Did you—Where did that—?"

"I bought it," he assured her. "Don't worry. I didn't pinch it from the cellar."

"I've never had it." She took a glass and sniffed it nervously.

"It's wine. You don't have to drink it, but I thought you might like it."

She took a tiny sip and looked at him in amazement. "You bought this? How can you afford such stuff?" Another sip.

Kit poured his own. He'd decided he liked champagne while with Lord Percy, who was wont to leaving unfinished bottles sitting around, and wave his hand and say Kit should have the rest. Lord Percy was usually blue-gilled when he said it, but he never flew into a temper the next day. Even a bit flat, champagne was fine stuff, and Kit had decided it was a hard-earned benefit of working for him.

Now he sat down on the wide ledge, with his back

against the chimney. There was just room for two people out here, and his feet dangled off into space, some forty feet from the ground.

Jennie sat beside him, tucking her skirts around her. "'Tis beautiful out here."

"It is." He watched her from the corner of his eye. Since coming to London she'd started wearing her hair differently. It showed off her lovely neck and her perfectly adorable ears.

She glanced at him and smiled. "Thank you for all your help," she said shyly.

"Anyone could tell you where to buy stockings."

"I know," she whispered. "But I prefer to ask you. I hope you don't mind."

"I prefer it above you asking anyone else."

They sat for a moment in blissful companionship. Jennie was so easy to be with, so warm and kind. She never nattered at anyone, or pestered or harangued. Martha, hired from the register-office, had remarked on how friendly Jennie was for a lady's maid.

"Are you pleased with Mr. St. James?" she asked after a few minutes.

His brows went up. "Yes."

She sipped her wine. "Then you expect to keep working for him for a long time?"

"I hope to." He did. Not only was St. James a decent fellow, he paid good wages, on time. Kit had been able to put aside a small sum just since starting with him.

And then there was that other reason, the one Kit would not say aloud. Not yet. He thought Jennie was fond of him, but he wasn't sure it was more than her ordinary engaging manner, and he didn't presume anything. *You're not a tomcat, young man, don't be acting like one,* his mother used to tell him.

"Why do you ask?" he dared inquire.

Even in the twilight he could see her blush. "No reason! Most of us at Perusia have been with the Tates forever. I didn't know how you might feel in Marslip."

Well now. To Marslip, he was indifferent. The Tates and St. Jameses were perfectly decent. But Jennie...

Perhaps it was time to test his luck a little.

"Hoping I'll give notice?" he asked.

CHAPTER 7

"**N**o!" Jennie almost shrieked. Her heart thudded alarmingly. That was the very last thing she wanted. "Of course not," she managed to add more calmly. "I only wondered..."

She wondered why he had bought a bottle of champagne —expensive wine!—for the two of them. She wondered what he meant by inviting her to sit out here on the roof with him. They'd simply sat in the kitchen hall, talking and relaxing, on other nights the St. Jameses had gone out.

And she wondered how this fine London valet, accustomed to serving lords, could stay in a hamlet like Marslip. Not that she wanted him to leave—very much the opposite. But other girls had warned her about restless men, and she didn't want to be silly about him.

"What did you wonder?" His voice could be so soft, like warmed velvet.

Jennie melted a little inside when he spoke to her like that.

"I only wondered if you're satisfied with Mr. St. James, or

if you were anxious to find another place. Now that you're back in London, I'm sure you could—in a matter of hours, most like. And then you wouldn't have to go back to Marslip, with the terrible roads and no parks and only a handful of shops..."

He put down his glass and twisted to face her. "I don't want to leave Marslip."

"No?" Her voice squeaked with relief.

He smiled. "Never."

She blinked. Never?

"If I left, I'd miss you," he said in reply to her unasked question.

"Would you?"

"Yes."

She blushed again. "How much?"

His smile faded a little. His eyes were dark and intense. "*Too* much."

"Well." Her heart was throbbing with delight. "I'm glad. I'd miss you fiercely if you left."

"Would you really? Why?"

She nibbled her lip, and drank more champagne, and then just said it. "I'm right fond of you, you know."

His smile returned, blinding with happiness. He leaned forward, and Jennie met him halfway.

It was a soft kiss, the sort of kiss a girl could fall into and linger over for days at a time. His hands, large and strong but still elegant, cupped her jaw and Jennie almost swooned into him.

"Right fond, eh?" he breathed, his lips on her brow.

Jennie choked on a giggle. "Am I supposed to say I fancy you? Is that what you're after?"

He laughed softly, and drew her next to him, his arm

warm and comforting across her shoulders. "It is indeed. For I fancy you more than any other girl alive."

CHAPTER 8

Things were glorious after that.

Kit contrived to accompany Jennie whenever she had to visit the shops. Even running errands was delightful when he did so with Jennie's arm through his. He pointed out sights and people to her as they went, grinning at her wide-eyed interest.

He also found himself growing more fond of Marslip. Surely there it would be easier to find a quiet unobserved corner to steal another kiss. He was glad they were going home soon.

Even better, Kit was sure his mood mirrored his employer's. It was plain to see that Mr. and Mrs. St. James were warming to each other. That augured well for his future.

The only fly in the ointment was that Mr. St. James had a secret, potentially a dangerous one. Kit didn't know what it was, and frankly did not want to know. He was under orders to watch for any letters and deliver them personally and immediately to his employer, without letting anyone else in the household see them. Twice he was sent out on the spot to deliver replies. And once, he was sent to watch over Mrs. St. James and Jennie, who were inspecting shop premises.

He had no idea whom he was supposed to fight, but he was ready, if the bloke threatened Jennie or her mistress.

But nothing happened, and then they went home. Even that journey, in the coach with the luggage, was an adventure. He held Jennie's hand and they took turns laughing at passersby, flocks of sheep being driven to market, a stray cow in the road, even strange shapes in the clouds. It was hard to be bad humored around Jennie.

Ever.

In fact, just thinking about her made him happy.

He realized what it meant the morning he went to the master's bedchamber, a pitcher of hot shaving water in his hands, and found Jennie standing uncertainly outside the mistress's door. "She's not there," she whispered, wringing her hands.

Kit paused and leaned his ear against the wood. Soft murmurings—two voices—made him grin. "Come away," he whispered back, taking Jennie's hand and leading her downstairs. "They don't want us now."

St. James had won his lady's heart. Kit knew it the moment he finally set eyes on the man, a good two hours later than usual. He was in love.

Just as Kit was.

He began to think about a life here. The most heartening example, to his eyes, was Jennie's own parents, who were housekeeper and butler at Perusia Hall. Why couldn't he and Jennie be the same, sharing a snug suite of rooms and going about their work side by side?

Sometimes they talked, late at night, sitting on the landing between their rooms in Poplar House. Jennie would bring up cups of warm milk and Kit would build the fire in her tiny fireplace. She told him about her childhood, running errands for her mother around Marslip and learning her letters at the school for the Perusia factory workers' children. He told her about waiting with his mother and sister at the docks for his father's ship to arrive, and how jubilant they would all be for days when he was home, sharing trinkets from his journeys. They laughed at themselves and at each other, and then together when Mary shushed them.

It was perfect. It was true love. He wrote to his mother about Jennie and began rehearsing a proposal in his mind.

And then it all went horribly wrong.

CHAPTER 9

J ennie didn't realize anything until it had already happened. She was in the back kitchen, her arms full of laundry, when Mary rushed in, wide-eyed and breathless. "Mercy on us!"

"What?"

Mary fanned her face. "I don't know! Mr. St. James got a letter, which Lawrence promptly took away as is his manner. But when Mr. St. James came home, he read it, jumped on his horse, and rode out like the devil was after him!"

"What was in the letter?" Jennie demanded in surprise.

"Don't know. I think Mrs. St. James wants to know, too, she's out there badgering Mr. Lawrence about it."

Jennie dropped the laundry and ran for the front of the house. True enough, Kit stood outside, hands open in innocence, shaking his head at whatever Mrs. St. James was saying to him. Miss Bianca was demanding and had a temper, but she was never cruel, and she would understand Kit wasn't to blame.

When her mistress came inside, silent and ashen, Jennie rushed to attend her. "Is aught wrong?" she ventured.

The reply was a long time coming. "I don't know," said her mistress softly.

The house was quiet and tense that night. Miss Bianca didn't eat and refused to go to bed. Jennie sat on the upstairs landing with Kit, whispering nervously over the candle.

"Didn't he say anything?"

Kit had his head in his hands. "Just that he had to go to Stoke, posthaste."

Jennie bit her lip and put her hand on his arm. He seized it and threaded his fingers through hers.

"I hope he's back soon," he murmured.

But there was no sign of the master the next morning. Mrs. St. James sent Kit into Stoke to find him, or find out about him, but he brought back no good news—in fact, no news at all. St. James wasn't even in Stoke. He'd left and gone somewhere else.

Jennie had never seen Miss Bianca so quiet. Her face was like a mask, and she shut herself up in the parlor all day. Jennie found Kit in the kitchen. He had the jar of boot black in his hand and a pair of boots in front of him, but he wasn't moving. "You need to tell her all," she urged him.

"I did."

Jennie shook her head impatiently. "No, not about yesterday—*all*. Everything you know about him."

Kit's shoulders hunched. "He swore me to secrecy..."

"And now he's run off and left her, when she's finally fallen in love with him," Jennie exclaimed. She knew her lady well.

"He'll come back."

Jennie blew out her breath. "If you say. But I think you

ought to tell her everything, so you don't get any blame if he's involved in something wicked."

She needn't have argued. Mrs. St. James called for Kit later that day. When he came back to the kitchen later, Jennie was almost in tears, waiting.

"I told her everything," he said at once. "All I know, which isn't much." He looked at her with dark eyes. "I hope she won't sack me."

"Did she—?"

"No," he said at her horrified question. "But she wanted to know more than I could tell."

That night they sat up again, simply holding hands on the landing. Jennie knew as well as he did that without a gentleman in the house, there was no need for a valet. And now that Kit had confessed to keeping secrets from her, Miss Bianca might not be keen to keep him on in any other capacity.

"She'll forgive him," Jennie said quietly but confidently. "I know her. As long as he comes home and has a reason, she'll forgive. Him *and* you."

"I hope you're right," was all Kit could reply.

CHAPTER 10

It was Ellen who brought the news the next night. She burst into the kitchen, breathing hard from running down the hill, and cried, "Mr. St. James has brought a madwoman into the house!"

Jennie tore off her apron and raced to Perusia Hall to get the full story from her mother. The whole house was in uproar, but Jennie got bits of information from her parents. She hurried back to tell Kit, who had been upstairs when Ellen made her hysterical announcement.

"The woman is his aunt," she reported. "She looks mad but Mrs. Bentley told Mam she might just be ill. Mrs. St. James received her very kindly, and Mam thinks she'll forgive Mr. St. James, seeing how unwell his aunt is and how abused she was."

"That's good news," exclaimed Kit. "He had good reason to go!"

Jennie nodded. "She'll understand. She'll rip up at him, mind, for frightening her so."

Kit laughed—in pure relief—and before Jennie knew it

she was in his arms, despite Mary's raised brows and Cook's knowing smile.

All Jennie's predictions came true over the next few days. The St. Jameses stayed at Perusia Hall with the poor woman, who was called Mrs. Croach. Ellen persisted in thinking her mad, but Jennie's mother wasn't so sure. And either way, the St. Jameses were reconciled, so Kit's position looked secure once more.

He proposed a few days later, in the afternoon while their employers were at the factory. With Cook's assistance, he lured Jennie out into the meadow beyond the stone wall of the yard, where the sun shone brightly and the field was lush with wild heather.

"What is it?" she kept asking. Kit just smiled and led her onward until they reached the large poplar tree that gave the house its name.

"Here's what it is," he told her, taking her hand and clasping it against his heart. "I love you, Jennie. I can't imagine life without you. I want to marry you, if you fancy me enough for that."

She blushed. "Mr. Lawrence!"

He waited, grinning like an idiot, his heart thumping madly.

"I do fancy you, more than enough for that," she said, her eyes sparkling. "Yes, I will."

With a whoop he swung her off her feet—a little too hard, as they ended up sprawled in the heather, laughing in each other's arms. It seemed a perfect moment for a kiss, although neither could say who kissed whom first.

"Kit," said Jennie sometime later, as they lay contentedly in the warm grass, "we'll have to ask—"

"I know." He grinned. "And I already asked your father

and your mother if they approve of me, which I thought a far higher bar than getting Mr. St. James's permission. He's in a benevolent mood right now, if you haven't noticed."

Jennie smiled, her cheek on his shoulder. "If Mam approves of you, the rest will be easy."

He kissed her again, then helped her to her feet. "I intend to ask Mr. St. James tonight."

When he heard the door a few hours later, Kit was still grinning. He winked at Jennie and loped up the back stairs. Mr. St. James had always been generous and fair to him. Mrs. St. James was very fond of Jennie as well. Surely neither of them would be opposed, if he and Jennie both wished it.

He reached the landing upstairs before his employer, and instantly knew something was off. It was his step, heavy and slow on the wooden stairs, as if he had to work to put one foot in front of the other. Kit paused, his confidence suddenly shaken.

Then St. James came around the bend in the stairs, head down, and Kit's heart plummeted. God's eyes. Something was very wrong.

The man looked up, and for a moment their gazes met before St. James looked away. Now Kit's heart nearly stopped. He'd seen that expression before. Lord Percy had looked at him just so, after that disastrous night in Vauxhall.

His face carefully blank, St. James nodded and went into his bedchamber. He stopped so suddenly that Kit, following behind, almost ran into him. He stepped neatly to the side, saving the collision, and spied what had stopped St. James.

There was a chocolate cup on the bureau. Madam must have brought it up this morning, after breakfast.

That happened regularly now. Kit and Jennie had learned to avert their eyes and their attention whenever the St.

Jameses went upstairs together. But both he and Jennie had missed clearing away that cup, and now the master was looking at it with stricken eyes. Kit silently cursed.

Quickly he moved forward and snatched it from the bureau, hiding it behind his back. "So sorry, sir. Will you—?"

"No," said St. James, sounding strangled. "I won't need you tonight, Lawrence."

Damn. Kit's bad feeling promptly burst into full-blown dread. "Not at all, sir?" he asked, praying to be told no, it was only a headache or a problem at the factory, and his employer would want a bath or a glass of port later.

"No," St. James repeated, his face averted. "Not at all. Take the evening free."

Kit let himself out and closed the door. For a moment he just stood there, clutching the wayward cup. His mind ran in a dozen directions at once, none of them happy. What had happened? Was it something he'd done? The trouble over Mrs. Croach seemed to have blown over, and the St. Jameses had been happier than ever—Kit had quickly learned never to enter a room without tapping and getting permission, to avoid interrupting a romantic moment.

Slowly he went back down the stairs. Had they fought? Had something happened to Mrs. Croach? Where was Mrs. St. James?

"Well?" Jennie demanded eagerly, eyes shining, as he stepped into the kitchen. Her question made him start, and then it almost made him sob.

"Something's wrong." Gently he set down the cup.

Jennie jumped to her feet, her mending falling on the floor. "What? Is Mr. St. James injured?"

He thought a moment. "Yes. In here." He touched his chest.

Jennie blinked, her brow knit in that endearing puzzled way.

Mary looked up, interested now. "'Tis his heart? Has he suffered a fit?" she asked in surprise.

Kit shook his head. "Not that kind of hurt. He looks... devastated."

"Oh no," exclaimed Jennie. "Perhaps Mr. Tate refused to produce that new Fortuna pottery—you know how much both of them have been working at it. Or perhaps his aunt suffered a relapse..."

Kit closed his eyes. He just knew it was neither of those things. The poor fellow looked shattered.

Jennie's arms went around him. "There now, Kit," she cried softly. "You look fair stunned! Sit down." She urged him into the chair next to hers and gave Mary a stern look. With a roll of her eyes, the maid gathered up her mending and left the room. "What happened?"

Kit looked into her dear, beautiful face. Perhaps he could beg a position in the factory. There wasn't much other employment in Marslip, but he would take anything— anything at all—to stay nearby. The innkeeper at the Two Foxes in Stoke was a decent chap, perhaps he needed someone to tend the taproom. "I think I'm going to be sacked," he told Jennie.

Her dark eyes widened. "What? No! Why would you be?"

Kit shook his head. "The look on his face. Something terrible's happened, and the last time a master looked at me that way, I was on the street the next day." *Without wages*, he didn't add. Please God at least let Mr. St. James pay his wages due.

Jennie sat bolt upright, still gripping his hands. "What? Never! I'll go to Mrs. St. James, she won't let that happen."

Kit looked at her. Mrs. St. James was made of stern stuff, but if Mr. St. James left, no one would need a valet at Poplar House. "Jennie... would you marry me anyway?"

She laughed. "Don't be silly, Christopher Lawrence. You're not going to be out on the street."

"If I have to take employment in Stoke, would you still marry me?"

Her laughter faded, and she grew somber. "Yes," she said. "You know I would."

The tightness in his chest eased. He smiled. "Then I'll be fine," he told her. "As long as you'll still have me."

From the front of the house came the sound of the door being flung open, and footsteps running upstairs. Mrs. St. James was calling her husband's name. Kit gripped Jennie's hand, hoping they made up, fearing things were about to get worse.

"I'd better go see if she needs me." Jennie pulled loose and darted to the stairs.

"No!" Kit lunged after her, but she was already on her way up, skirts in both hands. Despairingly he ran after her, trying to keep his steps quiet. "I don't think she'll want you just now," he whispered as he caught her at the top of the stairs.

Jennie put a finger to her lips and pressed open the door a few inches. Mr. St. James's bedroom was only a few feet away, and raised voices were clearly audible from it.

"God help me," breathed Kit, slumping against the wall. A furious quarrel with his wife would hardly improve Mr. St. James's mood.

Jennie turned and put her whole hand over his mouth. To his astonishment, she was grinning, her eyes sparkling. "Listen to 'em," she whispered.

Kit heard shouting. He'd *never* heard Mr. St. James shout.

His beloved put her cheek against his. "All will be well, Kit," she breathed in his ear. "Miss Bianca clears the air with a good row."

He pulled her hand away. "He looked *miserable*."

She grinned again and put her arms around his neck. "Aye, and listen to what they're saying to each other."

Kit fell silent and strained his ears. "...And if you think you're going to invalidate our marriage, *you're* mad, and I'll fight it till the end of my days because we belong together!" That was Mr. St. James, roaring louder than Kit had ever heard him. Mary in the kitchen could probably hear him.

"That's the first sensible thing you've said tonight!" was his wife's equally loud reply.

And then there was silence.

Jennie kissed him. "Let's go back down. We're *really* not wanted now."

Kit grinned and let her take him by the hand back down to the kitchen.

Mary stood clutching her mending, looking upward in amazement. "Are they fighting?" she asked in wonder.

"Not anymore," said Jennie saucily. "Don't go up unless someone rings, aye?"

Mary choked on a laugh. "Bless me, no! Not for anything!"

Kit pulled her around the corner, into the hall, out of sight of the kitchen. He took her in his arms and kissed her— just as, he strongly suspected, his master was doing upstairs to his own beloved. "Have you got a dress to be married in?"

She blushed, her hands clasped at the back of his neck. "I do. Miss Bianca gave me her beautiful burgundy gown. She said she'd got so many new ones in London, she wanted me to have that one."

"You'll look prettier in it than she does," he declared. "I love you, Jennie. Are you really going to marry me?"

"As soon as the banns are read." She kissed him. "You're my heart's desire, Kit Lawrence."

CHAPTER 11

In the end, she wore an even better dress to her wedding. When Kit finally spoke to Mr. St. James, the day after the furious shouting argument that ended in promising silence, Mrs. St. James had exclaimed that Jennie must have a new gown of her very own if she was to be married, and helped her choose the fine pink fabric. Three weeks later, Jennie came down the aisle on her father's arm, happier than any person had a right to be, to stand beside Kit and recite her vows.

Both the St. Jameses declared themselves delighted and gave Kit and Jennie time free for a honeymoon trip. Kit told her he had one planned, but he refused to reveal where.

"Trust me," he said as he started the gig.

Jennie rolled her eyes, waving her whole arm at her parents, her neighbors, her employers, her cousins—including Ellen, whose demeanor had markedly improved once Miss Cathy returned. Now Miss Cathy was Mrs. Mayne, the curate's wife, which had restored Ellen's pride and good humor. "You're a terrible tease," Jennie told her new husband.

"I want to take you on an adventure," he protested. "It can't be to Spain or America, but we have to start somewhere."

They were leaving Marslip. Not forever, but it did feel like the two of them were embarking on a grand adventure, together. She put her hand in his pocket and leaned against his shoulder. "Anywhere with you is a grand adventure for me."

He laughed. "Anywhere you are, *I'm* home."

It was the happiest honeymoon ever enjoyed in Liverpool.

THANK YOU FOR READING!

If you enjoyed the story, I hope you'll consider leaving a review or rating online to help other readers.

If you would like access to special previews, exclusive giveaways, and my very latest news, join my VIP Readers list at www.CarolineLinden.com. New members get a free exclusive short story as a welcome gift.

ABOUT THE AUTHOR

Caroline Linden was born a reader, not a writer. She earned a math degree from Harvard University and wrote computer software before turning to writing fiction. Since then the Boston Red Sox have won the World Series four times, which is not related but still worth mentioning. Her books have won the NEC Reader's Choice Award, the Daphne du Maurier Award, the NJRW Golden Leaf Award, and RWA's RITA Award, and have been translated into seventeen languages. She lives in New England.

ALSO BY CAROLINE LINDEN

Made in the USA
Middletown, DE
15 July 2022